TOILET

TUDOR TANGLE

BY
STEVEN VINACOUR

AWARD PUBLICATIONS LIMITED

ISBN 978-1-78270-385-3

First published by Award Publications Limited 2021

Published by Award Publications Limited,
The Old Riding School, Welbeck,
Worksop, S80 3LR

www.awardpublications.co.uk

21-958 1

Printed in the United Kingdom

WARNING:
CONTAINS TOILET HUMOUR!

CHAPTER 1

The class on stage had just finished their assembly telling the rest of the school how much they'd learned about butterflies (or, come to think of it, it might've been about Florence Nightingale or even about things you find in ponds – I wasn't really listening, and a quick glance around the hall showed me that neither was anyone else, including two teachers who had fallen asleep and were both **snoring** loudly). The class waited expectantly for a clap or at

5

least some sort of acknowledgement, but the entire hall was silent, until one of the boys started **picking his nose** with great enthusiasm.

(When I say picking, he was digging like a pneumatic drill digs up a road.)

Giggling turned to laughter as he continued to dig further and further, deeper and deeper. I thought at one point, his finger was going to come wiggling out of his ear! Slowly but surely all the other students noticed and all the attention had turned from the other children on stage to the busy boy with a digit up his nostril. The giggling got louder and louder until eventually our head teacher Mr Munford stepped in.

'Well, what a fascinating assembly. We all enjoyed it and learned a lot about the pyramids of Egypt.'

Oh! It was about the pyramids of Egypt?

I literally had no idea!

The head teacher continued, 'You've all worked very hard, and I think the whole school has learned something new.'

'I didn't, but then I'm more... picky,' shouted Martin Harris, the school bully. Everyone laughed. Some because it was a funny thing to say given recent events, and some because they didn't want Martin to PUNCH them on the nose when he saw them next.

'Yes, thank you, Martin, you've earned yourself a DETENTION for shouting out!' snapped Mr Munford. Martin looked annoyed.

'Now, before you go back to class I have a couple of announcements to make. Blah,

7

blah, blah ...' He didn't actually say blah, blah, blah (although I wish he had – that would've been brilliant!), but the things he said are not worth telling you (most of them were not worth telling me, and I go to that school!). But, then he surprised us all by finishing the assembly with a very interesting bit of information.

'... and that's why this year, for the first time in our school history, there will be a prom. There will be live music ...'

Everyone cheered.

'... there will be a photo booth ...'

Everyone cheered again.

'... and there will be excellent food provided by our school dinner ladies.' Everyone booed.

'That's enough. That's very rude of you all. Our dinner ladies work very hard to make sure you don't go hungry,' said Mr Munford.

'Well it looks like it hasn't worked for him!' shouted Martin Harris, pointing to the nose-picking boy who was just removing his nose-picking finger from his mouth. **EWWWW!**

'Detention all this week, Martin!' **hollered** Mr Munford. 'Now, all of you, go back to your classrooms quietly!'

We filed out of the hall making as much noise as we could. Because we are kids and it's what we do.

We all piled back into our classroom and waited for our teacher to follow. Someone called my name and I was just about to answer when...

HOLD **IT!** PAUSE THE STORY. NOBODY

MOVE! EVERYONE STAY EXACTLY
WHERE YOU ARE. BRACE YOURSELVES.
SOMETHING INCREDIBLE IS ABOUT
TO HAPPEN!!!
READY?
OK, HERE IT IS…

Chloe, the best-looking girl in the
school, was walking towards me. Chloe and
I had been getting on really well lately. I had
to pause the story because, well if Chloe
needs to speak to me then it's bound to
be really important or maybe she just
wants to hang out with me and chill out,
you know? Hold on. Here she is now. Deep
breath, here we go…

'Hey,' she says.
'Hey,' I replied.

... and she walked off.

Good, well that went well. Nice chat. Friendly, upbeat. I admit it could've been a little more ... well, just a little more would've been better, but, you know ... I see it as a positive step in the right direction.

So, where was I before Chloe and I hung out?

(Who's laughing? Are you laughing? We spoke and for a few moments we hung out. So, technically I'm correct. WHO'S LAUGHING NOW, EH? Oh, it's still you.)

When you have finished laughing at me and are prepared to be *sensible* and accept that Chloe clearly likes me and that we are destined to be together, then you can come and join me at the beginning of the next chapter. Until then, you stay

right here and think about your attitude.

CHAPTER 2

Back in the classroom, Miss Makeshift waited until we were settled and quiet and then told us a bit more about the prom.

'This will be a very special night. You will all have to dress up smartly in suits and dresses, there will be a DJ, dancing, a buffet meal and a prize for the prom king and queen. It is traditional for students to invite each other to be their prom date,' she giggled.

The whole class erupted into

laugher and banter: the girls teasing
each other about who would invite who,
and the boys claiming they weren't going if
they had to ask a girl to go with them (the
usual, mature classroom conversations!).
Eventually, Miss Makeshift quietened
everyone down.

I looked over at the love of my life, Chloe
Onions - yes, OK, if you haven't read my
previous story, her surname is Onions, as
in Onions. And, like the vegetable she makes
me cry, because she is so beautiful,
but unlike the vegetable she isn't round
and smelly! (Actually, that sounded really
weird, I'd like that to be removed from
this book and for all readers to forget that
I said anything about Chloe being round
and smelly.) Where was I? Oh yes, she is
beautiful and one day we will get married.

But, before that, I've got a prom to think about, and to make sure everything goes perfectly, I think I am going to need a plan.

THE PLAN

- **Create a plan** (done – see 'The Plan' above (labelled 'THE PLAN')).
- **Travel back in time to a time and place where I can learn how to dance and be the perfect prom date.** (Requires some research.)
- **Invite Chloe to be my prom date.**
- **Hire suit** (could wear Dad's old suit but don't want to look like I'm wearing Dad's old suit, and the problem with Dad's old suit is that it's Dad's old suit and therefore will definitely look like Dad's old suit).
- **Be crowned prom king alongside**

15

Chloe, who will be Prom queen.

- **Marry Chloe.** (Just so you know, this is for the future. I'm still at school so marriage is definitely not on the cards just yet, but it should be part of the plan – it's ALWAYS part of every plan.)

I was just finishing off my school lunch – a sandwich, as usual. I didn't want a sandwich but this is what happened:

Me: What's for lunch?

Dinner lady: Bolognaise

Me: Ooh, sounds good. Is it nice?

Dinner lady: Dunno, not tried it. The other dinner lady, Sandra, had it.

Me: Oh, I'll ask her then. Where is she?

Dinner lady: She went home sick. Food poisoning.

Me: I'll have a sandwich.

I took another bite and looked up to see my best friend, Ollie. He was carrying a tray of food. He loves school dinners. Today, he'd opted for **orange stuff with green bits** for main course and green stuff with orange bits for dessert. Ollie came rushing straight over to me, carefully balancing his tray and chewing the end of a pencil (which looked slightly tastier than the school lunch he'd chosen). Ollie doesn't rush very often, nor does he like to keep fit. He gets tired running a bath.

HAHA, good joke! **HIGH-FIVE!**

Don't leave me hanging!

Why are you leaving me hanging?

(Fine, suit yourselves.)

Ollie was trying to tell me something while attempting to catch his breath. All I heard was this:

'There's ... puff ... pant ... some ... puff ... pant ... **cough** ... one ... puff ... pant ...'

'What are you saying?' I asked, trying to understand him. 'Something about some pants that have made you cough? They sound like an awful pair of pants. Perhaps they are too tight? I suggest you stop wearing them immediately,' I said helpfully and went back to picking at my soggy sandwich.

Eventually, he caught his breath, stood up straight and calmed down enough to deliver some SHOCKING news.

(If you are a nervous person then I'd look away now, although, if you look away you aren't going to be able to read the shocking news and it's kind of key to the story so, I suggest putting your hand over your eyes and just peeking through your fingers. Anyway, here goes with the news...)

'I've just overheard, Stuart Hants is also going to ask Chloe to the prom!'

'What!!???' I said, not believing what I'd just heard. 'Stuart Hants? *The* Stuart Hants? A.k.a. Stu Hants? A.k.a. Stu Hants Poo Pants? He pooed his pants.'

(Just to that you know, I don't think Stu Hants did actually poo his pants. It's more a rhyming thing than factual. But, I was a desperate man so...)

'There is no way that Chloe would choose Stu Hants Poo Pants over me... Is there?' I asked, slightly concerned of the answer I'd get back. If she goes with him then she might fall in *love* and they might be together forever and get married and she would be known as Chloe Poo Pants which is even worse than Onions – which isn't bad...please don't tell her I said that!

'Well, he can dance, properly, and so can Chloe. If Chloe wants to be voted the prom queen, she will have to dance with her partner and you won't stand a chance of dancing with her.'

'What are you talking about? I can dance! I am an awesome dancer,' I argued, feeling a little hurt that my best friend should even question my dancing abilities.

'Being able to join a conga line is not dancing, Ted,' said Ollie as he smirked and fake conga-ed out of the school canteen.

'Anyone can conga!' I shouted. To prove the point, I too started to conga towards the door. Except as I kicked one leg out, I stubbed my toe on a chair and fell to the floor, rolling in agony. The dinner lady walked over and looked down at me.

'You didn't have the bolognaise, did you?' she asked, prodding me with the toe of her shoe.

'No,' I groaned.

'Oh, good. **Phew!** I thought you'd eaten it and then died. I didn't fancy explaining *that* to the headmaster... not again anyway.' She smiled to herself and walked off whistling a tune.

'Wait! What? What do you mean *"again"*?' But she had disappeared into the kitchen.

Later on that day, after school finished, Ollie came back to my house to hang out. We were both sitting quietly on my bedroom floor, deep in thought. Finally, Ollie spoke. 'I've been thinking about your dancing. You need to watch Rudolf Nureyev.'

'Rudolf who now?' I asked. 'Doesn't he help fly Santa Claus around? I hardly think that a shiny-red-nosed, *magic reindeer* can help me bust out some moves! Ollie, seriously, there's a reason that none of the other reindeer let him join in the reindeer games and it wasn't because he was king of the dance floor!'

Ollie sighed. 'He's a Russian *ballet dancer.*'

'Ollie, reindeers can't do ballet. They have four legs and hooves for a start.'

'Rudolf Nureyev is a famous *ballet dancer.* He was one of the best dancers in the world. He was the one who made ballet acceptable and an important role for men.'

'How on earth do you know all that?' I asked.

'I have a photographic memory, I remember everything,' he replied.

'No you don't,' I argued.

'Yes I do.'

'All right then, how long have you had a photographic memory?' I asked.

'Ummm.' He thought, scratching his head. He looked at me sheepishly (and by that I mean that he looked a bit embarrassed and not that he was suddenly covered in wool, standing in a field, eating grass and saying 'baa').

'I thought as much! Anyway, when I hit the dance floor on prom night, performing two grande *pliés* followed by a *jeté* and then ending with a *pirouette*, it's not going to win me the title of prom king. I need to turn up, armed with a wicked waltz and a terrific tango to show I'm SOPHISTICATED, followed by a superb street dance to show how cool I am.'

'Or you could just shuffle from side to side and occasionally click your fingers. That's what I'm going to do.' Ollie smiled triumphantly whilst demonstrating his ridiculously basic dance routine.

Ollie's advice was useless – I had to learn how to dance, FAST. (And by that I mean I had to learn quickly – not dance FAST. Unless it's a really FAST dance in which case I should learn how to dance FAST, FAST! Anyway, it doesn't matter...)

There was only one thing for it: I needed to go to the toilet. Only my toilet can help me now – is a sentence that no one has ever said before...ever!

In case you haven't yet realised, I am able to **TRAVEL BACK IN TIME** via my toilet. I know, when it comes to superhero abilities it's a little questionable but I can, and so I do. That's all you need to know right now.

The BIG question is, where do I travel back to and what dance should I learn?

CHAPTER 3

The school bell **ringing**, to mark the end of the day, was a long time coming. I stared at the clock on the classroom wall, willing the hands to turn faster. They ignored me and continued to crawl round the clock face. *Eventually,* I heard the sweet sound of the bell, packed up my things and we all headed home.

I walked in through the front door of my house, immediately shedding my coat, bag and jumper as well as kicking off both my shoes and with a flick of my legs sending them in two different directions (my shoes, not my legs). One of my shoes skidded across the floor and landed at the feet of a *strange* man who was sitting in our kitchen drinking tea with my mum.

'Hello. Who are you?' I asked.

'Ted! That's very rude,' snapped my mum.

'Sorry, Mum,' I sighed. 'Who are you? *Please-and-thank-you*,' I said politely.

'This is Mr Billman. He is an estate agent,' explained my mum.

'And may I ask what he is doing here?'

'He's come to value our house. Your father and I are considering MOVING.'

'Wait! What?' I said, but what I really meant was...
WHAT?!

In fact, that's not even good enough.

I meant...

WHAT?!!

Actually, looking at that, it doesn't seem "what-y" enough, so, I think I'm going to have to up the "what-iness" to a...

WHAT?!!!

'No, no, no. We can't move and we are not moving. Thank you, **Mr Estate Agent** for coming round, but the Joneses are staying **RIGHT HERE,**' I explained whilst giving him his coat and briefcase and ushering him out the door.

Mum was losing her temper. *TERRY BARRY LARRY GARY HARRY*

JERRY PERRY LENNY BENNY JOHNNY TOMMY JULIE JONES!' she shouted.

The **estate agent** started looking around, confused. 'You have *twelve sons _and_* a daughter? All living here?'

'He's making fun of my name. Tell him to leave,' I said to my mum.

'I'm not making fun of you. I just thought it was strange.'

'He said I was strange, tell him to leave,' I whined.

'I didn't say you were strange, it was the situation.'

'He called me a situation, tell him to leave,' I moaned again.

'I didn't... look I... ' muttered the **estate agent.** 'I just thought there were a lot of children, that's all.'

'No, it's just me. I have a very long name and my parents can't make decisions, but I can and I have – we **AREN'T** moving house. Sorry to have wasted your time, Mr Gillman.'

'Billman,' he corrected.

'Pillman,' I replied.

'*Billman,*' he said.

'Dillman,' I replied.

'GILLMAN,' he said.

'Whatever. Have a nice day, Mr Chillman.'

'IT'S HILLMAN!' he shouted. 'I mean *Gillman. BILLMAN!!!* **AARRGGH!**' I heard him scream as I closed the door.

I watched him drive away. When he'd gone, Mum was standing in the hallway with her hands on her hips. She was just about to say something (probably tell me off) but I interrupted her.

'Mum, seriously, why would you want to move?'

'Well, we could do with more space. You could have a bigger bedroom.'

'I don't need a bigger bedroom. I have all the space I need. I like this house. We have to stay here.'

'Well, maybe you're right, maybe we should just update the kitchen and bathroom.'

'Sorry, what? Did you just say update the bathroom?'

'Yes, you know, get a new bath, sink and toilet. Something modern and smart.'

'NO! NO! NO!' I took a deep breath. 'Mum, you can't get rid of our toilet... it... it holds too many special memories for me,' I garbled, starting to panic.

'What are you talking about, Ted? Do you seriously have fond memories of past trips to the toilet?'

'Mum, I'm not talking about going to the **toilet.** I'm talking about things that happened in the toilet. It was where I had my **first bath** and my **first hair wash.** It was in that room that I remember sitting on my potty looking up at that giant toilet thinking that one day, **one day**, I'll be big enough to use it...'

Mum sniffed and a little tear ran down her face.

It was working, quick, carry on...

'I **love** our toilet. Look on the wall over here, that's where you made a mark to see how much I'd grown. And look at that toilet bowl – I still remember sitting there for my first poo. I felt **so proud** as I wiped my first bum.'

'Ted! That's **disgusting.** And to imply

you had a **first bum** means you now have a second bum, which is incorrect. Bums aren't like teeth – you don't lose one and get another.' Mum corrected unnecessarily, wiping her nose and looking cross again. However mad she got, she would always make time to correct my language skills.

'I heard Dad saying that Aunt Jackie had a **fabulous** new bum,' I argued.

'Oh, *did he?* I wondered why he suggested we should both go to her pilates class. I'll be having words with him later.'

'And will you mention to him that we **AREN'T** moving house or changing the bathroom?' I pleaded.

'I'll pass on your comments,' she sniffed and walked out of the room.

Good, so with the bathroom renovations/ moving house **CRISIS** temporarily halted, it was time for me to concentrate on the next crisis that I faced: learning how to DANCE.

CHAPTER 4

I need to do some proper research and find out where I can travel **BACK IN TIME** to. Which era was the first to dance? Who invented dance moves? Should I try classic dancing or MODERN? First, let's rule out the dancing styles that are not appropriate for school proms.

I need to draw a chart.

A Dancing Chart*

*please note that this chart doesn't actually dance

Style	Pros	Cons	
Tap	Chloe would hear me walking across the dance floor.	Everyone in the school would hear me walking across the dance floor.	X
Contemporary	It contains front flips, backflips, cartwheels and gymnastics. Chloe would be super impressed with that.	I can't do front flips, backflips, cartwheels or gymnastics.	X
Streetdance	It's cool, modern and bound to impress.	I need a crew. Ollie and I are not a crew. Although we could be a crew without a clue (which is funny, I'll write that down) (I just did).	X
Disco	It's called disco dancing so it must be the kind of dancing that you do at discos – this is worth exploring.		✓

Breakdancing	It's cool. Really, really cool. Chloe would instantly think I'm cool. Really, really cool.	It doesn't feel like you are actually dancing with someone when they are standing still and you are upside down or spinning on your back. Also, my cap would need to face backwards and Chloe might think I'm leaving when I'd only just arrived. ✗
Line dancing	It looks easy.	I am not a cowboy. ✗
Ballroom dancing	It's elegant, posh and Chloe would definitely be impressed.	I'm not so sure that elegant or posh accurately describes me. Although I did once extend my little finger whilst drinking a cup of tea – that's really posh, I'm sure of it. ✓
Morris dancing	HAHAHAHA....No!	.... just, NO! ✗

I jumped on my computer (not literally or I would've broken it) and started to search for famous dancers from the past. I thought the best idea was to start WAY BACK in time and then HEAD FORWARD so that I have a complete knowledge of dancing through the ages. That way, Stu Hants Poo Pants wouldn't stand a chance with his arm waving, clippy-cloppy, rubbish dancing skills.

I discovered that there were two queens of England (MARY I and ELIZABETH I) who both loved music and were very fond of dancing. Then I read that Elizabeth I forced her *ladies-in-waiting* to dance while she tapped out the rhythm with her foot. Well, that's why they are called *ladies-in-waiting* - they were waiting for ELIZABETH I to stop tapping her feet so they could stop dancing!

HAHAHA! It's a joke about ELIZABETH I – come on, you don't get that in a **Harry Potter** book!

Anyway, that wasn't for me, I wanted to learn to dance, not be **_made_** to dance. I continued to search the INTERNET. And then I saw it!

A cat playing the piano! Brilliant!

(But distracting...)

I needed to concentrate.

I carried on searching for a few minutes and then I heard a **knock** on my bedroom door.

'Ted, it's me!' called Mum through the door. 'Are you doing your homework?'

'Yes, Mum,' I lied.

'I've brought you a snack.'

'Excellent,' I said, getting up and

opening my door. Mum was standing there with a tray **full** of food. Classic Mum – can't make a decision.

'Wow! That's a **lot** of food!'

'Well, I wasn't sure what to make for you so I brought you a slice of watermelon, a pie, three plums, a sausage, a cupcake and a slice of cheese.'

'Have you been reading *THE HUNGRY CATERPILLAR* again?' I asked. 'If you could just get me a big green leaf, my tummy ache will be gone by Sunday.'

'Do you have a **tummy ache?** Oh no! I'll make you a cup of tea.'

'I don't have a tummy ache, Mum,' I said.

I should explain that my mother thinks that **everything** can be cured with a cup of tea. It's a good job that my mum isn't a nurse or this would happen.

CUT TO HOSPITAL. (*LOTS OF DOCTORS RUNNING AROUND.*)

Doctor: Quick, I need all available medical staff, there's been a terrible incident, hundreds of people will be arriving here and they will all need urgent medical attention.

My mum: I'll put the kettle on.

Anyway, back to my bedroom.

I finally convinced my mum that I didn't have a tummy ache and that she'd made too much food.

'Well, you know what I'm like,' laughed Mum. 'I can't make up my mind. Here, just eat what you want and leave the rest. I'll give it to your dad for dinner.'

I took the tray from my mum's hands, placed it on the floor and casually snacked on the fruit whilst surfing the web looking for the perfect era to travel back to.

I'd made up my mind to travel back as far as I could. I started to read about the 1500s and the reign of **Henry VIII.** It seems that he was famous for something other than having lots of wives (he had six). He also loved music and dancing. Perfect! It looks like I'll be going back to **Tudor** times.

In case you were wondering, back in **Tudor** times they didn't use numbers like we do today, they used Roman numerals.

$$X = 10 \qquad V = 5 \qquad I = 1$$

(So Henry VIII = Henry 5+1+1+1 = **Henry 8th**)

So, if you went down to the local shops in **Tudor** times you could buy a comic and a bag of sweets and the shopkeeper would say, 'That'll be VI pounds.'

And then you'd say, 'I only have IV pounds and XIV pence.' Or something like that... (Actually nothing like that, I made that bit up!)

Another thing I remembered from when we learned about the Tudors in school was that Henry VIII had lots of wives because some of them died and some of them he chopped their heads off (they also died of course – that's what happens if your head gets chopped off). There is a well-known poem that teaches you about what happened to his six wives. It goes like this...

DIVORCED
Beheaded
Died
DIVORCED
Beheaded
Survived

I have just decided to write a poem about my future wife...

Chloe, Chloe, Chloe Onions
Together we'd have lots of fun-ions
In the wind, the rain, the snow or sun-ions
And I'd never chop your head off like
Henry V one, one, one-ions.

Brilliant! Well, OK, it needs a little work but you try rhyming words with onions!

I've said before that I like to do as much research as I can before going **BACK IN TIME** so, here's what I found out about Henry VIII:

- Henry became king when he was **17** years old! He had his coronation on

24th June 1509. (Having a coronation means that he was made king and not that he had chicken and mayonnaise plopped onto his head.)

- Henry very nearly didn't become king because he had an older brother called **Arthur.** But, he died when he was 15 which means, if he had lived, then there would be no **Henry VIII,** no dancing and no chance of me ever impressing **Chloe,** and I would live the rest of my life alone with my one regret that I couldn't dance and therefore never found **true happiness.** (OK, I'm being over dramatic. I would've found someone else to teach me but now you see how important it is for me to impress Chloe — she is very **beautiful.** Did I mention that before?)

Reader: Yes. (Yawn.)

Me: You are very rude.

- Henry married six times. Three of his wives were called Catherine. (Here's another interesting fact. I don't know anyone called Catherine. What do you mean, 'that isn't interesting'? Do you know anyone called Catherine? Well there you go then.)

Right, back to my story.

I'm going on an adventure. QUICK, Get me to the toilet! (Is a catchphrase no superhero has ever said. Except maybe the time Spider-Man ate a dodgy sausage roll and... never mind.)

Look, of all the cool things that could've

been a **TIME-TRAVELLING** machine,
I got a toilet, but hey, it works, so I'm just
grateful. Batman has a cave, Superman
has a phone box, I have a toilet. Plus, the
good thing is that if I am about to start my
adventure and I suddenly need the toilet, I
can just go. Superman can't do that in his
phone box! (Although, having said that, the
one at the bottom of our road always smells
like someone has...)

Anyway, I'm digressing. To the 1500s –
Tudor times... let's go!

CHAPTER 5

I tiptoe to the **toilet** and lock the door. I kick off my slippers, lift the toilet lid and climb in.

BRRRRR! It's freezing! One day I'm going to invent a toilet that has **warm water** in, and **bubbles,** maybe some warm towels – actually I'm not – no one ever feels the temperature of the water in a toilet unless there is a very specific problem.

48

THE SPECIFIC PROBLEM

There is a **blockage** and they need to put their hand down there.

THE SOLUTION

Get a plumber to do it – they are used to it. Whoever does it should be wearing big, thick gloves and if they aren't then they should go and buy a pair.

THE SPECIFIC PROBLEM

They stand in the bowl with the intention of **TIME-TRAVELLING** and get cold feet.

THE SOLUTION

There is not a chance that you will be able to time-travel via **_your toilet_** so the solution is climb out of your toilet, dry your feet and stop being silly.

They get a bit of water splashed on their bum whilst sitting on the toilet possibly having a poo.

THE SOLUTION

Change your diet. Eat more **fibre**.

So, there you go, I'll put up with the cold water for the time being. Here we go.

I press the flush and say 'Tudor times' over and over. Freezing cold water rushes in and soaks my legs. I let out a quiet gasp as the icy water flows into the bowl and over my feet. I take a deep breath and slowly count to three. One, two, three. I start to spin. Slowly at first but **PICKING UP SPEED** with every turn. In a few seconds everything is spinning so fast it becomes a blur. **I CAN'T FOCUS ON**

ANYTHING – not the bath, the sink or my pink facecloth.

(Aarrgghhh! I've just revealed I have a pink facecloth. Ignore that.)

Round and round I spin, turning faster and faster until I'm whizzing round at a gazillion miles per hour and then **WHOOOSH!** There is a loud sucking noise and I disappear straight

D

O

W

N

the **toilet.**

I hold my breath as my body is pulled up and around the U-bend and then I'm flying down the biggest, **FASTEST** water slide in the world. I'm leaning left and right, up and down, under and over. The **ROAR**

of the gushing water is almost deafening.
I can't focus on anything apart from little
flecks of multi-coloured light. I **ZOOM**
down the tunnel of bright lights, never
slowing for a second. I brace myself for two
huge loop-the-loops that make my
stomach feel funny. But, there is no time to
concentrate on that as I pick up speed again.
Then I start my descent, turning down and
round, over and over again like being on a
helter-skelter, faster and **FASTER**
I turn round and round, further and
further down and then the slide suddenly
VANISHES beneath me and I float
into nothing. There is silence all around me.
I float like a boat, adrift on a perfectly still
pond. I relax as the excitement of the
ride slowly disappears and I start to calm
myself down. I drift around for ten minutes

or so which gives me plenty of time for my mind to wander.

(I start to think about why most songs are written about *love* rather than **SUSHI**. Sushi is much nicer and less complicated than love. There should be more songs written about **SUSHI**. I decide to write one there and then but I can't think of any words that rhyme with sushi - which is possibly why there are no songs about sushi.)

I close my eyes and **breathe deeply.** When I open them again I am curled up next to a giant wall made of rough stone. I look around. There are people running around like crazy. **CHAOS** is breaking out everywhere.

CHAPTER 6

As I try to make sense of my surroundings, a large, middle-aged lady wearing a long black dress approaches me. She has a crisp white apron tied tightly around her waist and a matching hat covers her hair. In her arms she carries a **huge** basket of bread.

'Come on, come on, there's no time to rest. Get up, you lazy young man, and take this to the banquet hall. **Come on, we are in a hurry!**' she screeched.

I leaped to my feet and grabbed the basket

of bread. It was big. Really big.

Way too big for me to carry on my own.

Who needs this much bread? I stagger

across the room and then two young women

carrying an even bigger silver tray piled

high with delicious-looking fruit run past me,

knocking into the basket. I lose my balance

and the bread rolls roll everywhere.

(Now I know why they are called rolls –
because they do indeed roll. It's the same
for baps as they do indeed... umm... err... bap –
scratch that. It's not the same for baps. Back to
the story...)

I groaned at the mess and staggered back
to my feet to retrieve the bread.

Suddenly the door flew open with a
CRASH and I was face to face with the
biggest man I had ever seen. He was half
man, half mountain.

He was a **MAN-tain!**

He had a huge bristly beard and was wearing a pile of gold chains, and rings on every finger. He looked just like **Hagrid** – if Hagrid gave up being a **wizard** and pursued a career in rap music. He saw me on the floor **surrounded** by bread rolls and bent down so that his face was just **inches** from mine. I could smell his hot breath as he spoke. It smelled like a mixture of fish, meat and jewellery. (Not as unpleasant as you'd think – I mean I wouldn't buy perfume made from it but as an air freshener it could work. My mum once bought one called **Ocean Stench** or something like that and it was way worse than this...)

I'm **kidding** – his breath was **disgusting!**

'**AND WHO ARE YOU?**' he boomed.

He was so loud that the whole room seemed to **SHAKE**. Everyone in the room froze in fright.

'T – T – T – Ted,' I stammered.

'Well, T-T-T-Ted. What are you doing?'

'Just picking up these,' I said showing him a bread roll. 'Oh, and it's only one T.'

'**WHAT?**' he bellowed

'One T,' I repeated.

'One T?' He paused. You could hear a pin drop.

'...'

(Clearly no one had a pin or maybe they had one but didn't drop it because they were frozen in fear – see above.)

Either way I didn't actually hear a pin drop but it was quiet enough to hear one **IF** someone did have one and at that moment decided to drop it (which they didn't).

Sorry, where was I? Oh yes.

'Your name is **Ted Wonty**?'

'No, my name is Terry Barry Larry Gary Harry Jerry Perry Lenny Benny Johnny Tommy Julie Jones.'

'What a silly name.' He laughed a big throaty **BOOMING** laugh. 'Well, whoever you are, I'm hungry. I want lunch. Hurry up and bring it to my chamber.'

The king turned on his heel and marched out of the room, slamming the door behind him. The moment the door **BANGED SHUT** everyone seemed to breathe out at the same time with relief and then continued running backwards and forwards. I sat on the floor mesmerised by the hustle and bustle.

Everyone that ran past me was carrying something. Meat, fish, flowers, a banana milkshake – hey, **wait a minute,** how was someone carrying a banana milkshake? They weren't invented until the 1800s.

"**Hey!**" I called after him. But he'd disappeared into the crowds of kitchen staff and servants.

Eventually a boy a little older than me helped me to my feet.

'Come on,' he said. 'You've got a job to do, I'll show you where the king's crockery is kept.'

'Is the king's crockery kept concealed?' I asked, wondering how far I could take this tongue-twister.

'The king's crockery is kept concealed in the kitchen with the cutlery,' answered the boy.

'How clean is the king's crockery, concealed in the kitchen with the cutlery?'

'*Completely* clean,' he snapped.

'So you can **confirm** that the king's crockery, kept concealed in the kitchen with the cutlery, is completely clean?'

'**Enough!** Stop talking!' he shouted. 'His Royal Highness doesn't like to be kept waiting. If he gets cross, he's been known to behead people.'

'I'm sorry,' I said. 'For a minute there I thought you said that if he gets cross he's been known to behead people.'

'Yes, I did say that.'

'Well, in that case, let's stop chatting about the king's Clean Crockery kept Concealed in the kitchen with the Cutlery, and Concern ourselves with keeping our kecks... I mean necks!'

I was starting to panic. I remember

reading that Henry VIII chopped off his **wives**' heads, but I thought I was safe as it was unlikely that I would end up marrying him. Now I discover he can decide to chop anyone's head off if the mood takes him.

We ran into the kitchen to collect the king's crockery.

(It was indeed kept clean and concealed... never mind, we found it – let's just leave it there.)

The boy showed me how to lay the cutlery and crockery perfectly on a highly polished silver tray. He **RUSHED** around plating up large cuts of meat.

'What is that?' I asked.

'Peacock and swan, the king's favourite lunch.'

'Ewww, that's **disgusting.** How could he eat such beautiful birds?'

'I don't question him, I just serve him whatever he wants and make sure I don't give him anything he doesn't want – like vegetables. King Henry hates vegetables.'

We speed-walked back to the king's room being extra careful not to drop or spill anything. The boy handed me the tray and gently pushed me into the room and towards the king.

Henry VIII eyed me suspiciously as I carefully placed the tray in front of him, bowed and double-checked that my head was still on my shoulders. (It was. Phew!) I poured a glass of wine and stood back.

The king leaned forwards and shovelled a forkful of roasted bird into his mouth. He chewed loudly as he continued to look at me with *suspicion.* He brought the glass of wine to his lips and sipped it making a noisy slurpy sound.

'A VERY GOOD LUNCH,' he boomed. 'VERY GOOD INDEED.'

'Thank you, Your Highness.'

'Peacocks and swans are both delicious. Royal birds – too good for peasants.' He nodded to himself.

'Yes, Your Highness. They are very posh, Your Highness,' I agreed.

'They aren't "posh", boy. Food isn't "posh", it's *extravagant* and *opulent*,' he said with his nose in the air.

'OooOOOooOh!' I said. Because that's what I always say when someone says impressively long words and I don't know what they mean. It covers up the fact that I have no idea what they are talking about.

'You have no idea what I'm talking

63

about, do you?'

'Oh, well...'

'It means *expensive* and *luxurious*,' he sniffed.

'OooOOOoooh!' I said again.

'Now you are just being silly. What was your name again, boy?'

'It's Terry, Barry, Lar... It's Ted, just Ted.'

'Ted? I see. Well, you've impressed me with your lunch-making abilities. Perhaps you could teach some of the other staff to make me meals fit for a king?'

'I could, I mean I'd be glad to, sir. Perhaps, in return you could teach me one thing?' I said, ignoring the fact that I hadn't actually cooked anything and if someone served me swan or peacock I'd politely decline and just have some toast and jam. However, I did have a perfect opportunity.

'And what might that be?' he asked, intrigued.

'To dance, Your Highness. I can't dance and I know you are an **excellent** dancer. Would you teach me?'

'Dance?' he bellowed. 'You want me to teach you... a peasant... to dance?'

'Well, that's a bit rude but yes, Your Highness.'

'Hmmm. You are a strange young man. Not many people ask me, Henry VIII, to do things for them. If they did I'd probably chop their heads off. They tend to just do things for me. Because I'm a king and they aren't. I don't have many friends.'

'Well, that's probably because of the... you know... the thing?'

65

'What?' he asked. 'What... "thing"?'

'You know... the whole chopping off heads thing you do.'

'Oh, that! Do you think that puts people off?'

'Well, it could do. I don't think the people whose heads you've chopped off are too happy about it and, well, you have chopped off a lot of heads.'

'Well, you say a lot. Only about 70,000 but they kind of deserved it.'

'Surely they didn't all deserve it. What did they do?' I asked.

'They disagreed with me,' he quipped, picking meat from between his teeth. Then, raising an eyebrow, he peered at me and said, 'You aren't disagreeing with me, are you?'

'No. No. No. I completely agree with

everything you've done so far. But... going forward, perhaps you could do it a bit ... *less* – in pursuit of the whole friend thing, you know?'

'Hmmm, the thing is I do rather enjoy chopping heads off. Have you ever tried it? **Wait!** Does it put you off me?'

'Well, I'll be honest, I do like my head where it is and would rather you didn't arrange for it to go anywhere else.'

'Right, I understand. No more chopping off heads if I want friends, eh? What about legs?'

'No, I think that might prevent people from getting too close to you too.'

'It would stop them running away, that's for sure. Arms?'

'No.'

'Hands?'

'No.'

'What about a finger – just the little finger. No one cares about them too much.'

'I think that if you want to make more friends, you have to **stop** chopping off anything at all. Completely. No more. Ever.'

'Hmmm. I see. Maybe you are right, maybe I will stop.' The king thought for a few moments until I interrupted the silence.

'Good. Now, the thing is, I need to learn to dance or Chloe will go to the dance with Stuart and not me.'

'I could chop Stuart's head off?'

'As much as that would solve the problem, I thought we had agreed that you weren't going to—'

'Yes, Yes. No more chopping off bits and pieces.'

'Good.'

'To be honest, I do feel a little like dancing. You see, I've just been told some good news. The thing is I've always wanted a male heir—'

'Me too! My dad says it will happen when I get a bit older and when my voice changes and I—'

Henry continued as if I'd never spoken. He leaned over to me, cupped his huge hand round his mouth and **whispered** in my ear. 'I've just been told that my wife is expecting a *baby*. A boy! I am OVERJOYED! Finally, I will have a son to raise to be the heir to the throne. Although, what I need is a good name. A strong, name that says, "I AM THE FUTURE KING".'

'Well, you are Henry VIII.'

'Yes.'

'The son of Henry VII?'

'Correct.'

'Who was the son of...'

'Yes, yes, yes. What's the point of your questions?'

'So, were you all called Henry?'

'Well, there are a lot of Henrys, yes.'

'The royal family really like the name Henry, don't they?'

'I suppose they do rather, yes.'

'It's not very... *different*, is it? I mean, you've had a few Henrys, what about naming him Gary, Wayne or Justin?'

'Or what about... Henry... Henry is a great name.'

'Yes,' I sighed. 'Or Henry.'

'Good, that's decided then. Wait, what's your name?'

'Ted.'

'Short for Edward, eh?'

'Actually it's short for Terry Barry Larry Gary Harry Jerry Perry Lenny Benny Johnny Tommy Julie Jones.'

He looked at me with a confused expression on his face. 'That's a very silly collection of names. Fine, not Henry then, but what about Edward? I like Edward. Edward is an excellent name. I shall call my son Edward. After you, my new friend.'

'I'm very flattered, sir, but my name isn't—'

'Are you disagreeing with me? You know I don't like it when people disagree with me. I tend to get all... choppy.'

'No, Your Highness. Honestly I—'

'I'm joking! If we are going to be friends then you have to learn to lighten up, Edward.' The big man roared with laughter.

'Edward is an excellent name. Which is why it's my name. Always has been. People always say to me, "Hey, Edward, how are you today?" and I say, "I, Edward (because that's my name), am good." Because I have the name Edward.' I gulped and looked up at the king who glared back at me. Eventually his face softened. He stood up and clapped his hands together loudly.

'I wish to dance with Edward, my new friend. Where are my musicians?' he bellowed.

A huge door swung open and men and women dressed in gold robes filed into the room. Each person carried a musical instrument. I saw trumpets and cornets (the musical type, not the type you put ice cream in. Although that would've been really nice as it was quite hot in there. Unfortunately

72

for me, although ice cream was introduced
to **Henry II** of France by his Italian wife,
it wasn't until 1660 that ice cream was made
available to the public, and years after that,
that someone thought to stick it in a cone, bite
the end off and suck it through... mmm...
delicious).

Where was I?

The musicians continued to fill up the
room. Each of them carried an instrument,
including a collection of large and small
string instruments. One person had a harp
which was so **BIG** that they had to sit
down and hold it between their legs to stop
it falling over! There were also two men who
played the lute, which is like a guitar only it's
a bit... erm... lute-y-er. (I don't actually
know what a lute is. I would look it up online
but, you will have realised by now that I'm in

Tudor times and the INTERNET connection wasn't great during that period.)

One of the players gave a polite little cough and they started playing *beautiful* orchestral music. Henry smiled. 'Now, my friend, do you prefer the *pavane,* the *galliard* or the *almain?*'

'Oh, no thank you. I've just eaten,' I politely answered.

Henry **LAUGHED** loudly. 'They are dances, boy. Come. Stand up. Watch me closely. I'll teach you.'

CHAPTER 7

We danced for what seemed like hours. Henry was an excellent teacher. He stamped his feet or clapped his hands in time with the music and *BARKED* orders at me.

'Keep in time.'

'Stop tripping over your own feet.'

'Arms, *ARMS!* Move your arms!'

'Listen to the rhythm of the music.'

'... and dab!' (I'm kidding, Henry VIII did NOT know how to dab!)

The musicians played beautiful music non-stop. As we danced, he told me all sorts of interesting things about being the **KING OF ENGLAND**. Some of it I'd already learned in school. We'd studied **Henry VIII** and the **Tudors** last term but, I had to be super careful I didn't reveal anything that hadn't happened yet.

'Hey, Henry, you know your ship, the Mary Rose, that you've only just launched and are really, really proud of. Well it sinks in 1545. Be careful. Bye.'

'Hey, Henry, I don't want to be the bearer of bad news or anything but, let's just say, I wouldn't make too many plans after 21st April 1509.' (That's the date of his death, by the way.)

As I danced, I suddenly realised that of all the King Henrys, **Henry VIII** was the most famous. One of the main reasons he was so famous was because he liked **chopping** his wives' heads off. But what about all the other Henrys? Surely they did something nicer than that – things that they should be famous for? I decided that when I got back home, I'd make a chart of things that the other **King Henrys** had done. And I did, so here it is... (I completely understand that the period of time is confusing right now. So, just to explain: I am in the **past,** thinking about the *future* – which, for me, is actually the **present** – and I'm talking from the **past** about doing something in the *future,* which is here now in your **present.** I hope that has cleared it up.)

List of King Henrys

By Terry Barry Larry Gary Harry Jerry Perry
Lenny Benny Johnny Tommy Julie I*

(*I as in 'the first', not I as in me)

Henry I   (Born 1068) His father was William
the Conqueror (because he was
famous for conquering things*) and his
sister was called Adela* (Famous for
getting to number one in the charts
with 'Rolling in the Deep'**)

*True   **Not true

Henry II   (Born 1189) Also known as Henry
Curtmantle, Henry Fitz Empress
or Henry Plantagenet. Sometimes
known as Count of Anjou, Count of
Maine, Duke Of Normandy and Count
of Nantes. Sometimes known as Lord
of Ireland — probably not that famous
because no one knew what to call him!
Although if I ever write a detective
series, I would call them Curtmantle
and Fitz. They sound super cool!

78

Note to self: Write a best-selling series of books based on two detectives called Curtmantle and Fitz. Give Curtmantle a quirky moustache that he fiddles with when he's thinking and give Fitz big hair and a limp.

Henry III (Born 1207) Owned an elephant, a leopard and a camel. Which is pretty cool. I'd like an elephant, leopard and a camel but I'm not prepared to clear up after they've pooped. I mean, how big would the poop bags have to be?

Henry IV (Born 1367) Was the first King of England to speak English rather than French. So if it weren't for him I'd have to write this book in French, which would be a massive problem as I don't speak French.

Henry V (Born 1386) Went to war with France, a war that lasted 100 years – I imagine that everyone was very tired by the end.

Henry VI   (Born 1421) Became king at 9 months
            old*. Introduced laws including
            compulsory nappy changes, banquets
            of mushy food and insisted on
            compulsory time-out for dummy
            sucking.**
            *true   **not true

Henry VII   (Born 1457) He invented the English
            money system but then got greedy
            and wasted lots of it. He bought
            a gold lute for his daughter (see
            above, I still don't know what a lute
            is but now I've learned it comes in
            gold, which is nice). He also bought
            a lion for his wife. I'm not sure
            my mum would like Dad to buy her a
            lion, and when I marry Chloe I don't
            think she would like it if I bought
            her a lion — although it would scare
            Sandra Wum away!

Suddenly, the king stopped dancing
and faced me. 'Well, boy, I have thoroughly

enjoyed teaching you to dance. You have potential and you are an excellent student. But now I am tired. When I get tired I get grumpy, and when I get **GRUMPY,** I get the urge to chop off a head.' He suddenly grabbed me by the collar. 'GUARDS, get me my favourite head-chopping axe!'

I was too stunned to say anything.

Wait! What was happening? I thought we were friends? Although, I instantly made up my mind that I didn't want to be friends with anyone who claimed to have a favourite head-chopping axe! My best friend, Ollie, has a favourite plate and I think he has a preference for a specific spoon, which I think is weird, but at least it isn't dangerous. Anyway, where was I? Oh yes. AARRRGGGHHH! The king's bad mood! An axe! My head!

Perhaps if I could put him in a good mood it might help.

'Wait, Wait!' I shouted. The king raised his hand and everyone stood silent and still.

'Umm... where should Henry VIII go if he needs help learning English?'

The king looked confused. 'I don't know. Tell me where should I go if I need help learning English?'

'To an English Tudor – as in English tutor... get it? Tudor? Tutor?... No...?'

It was a great joke – feel free to use it when you are at school, but only if you want to be named the funniest person in the class. (OK, fair enough. Under the *circumstances* it was a great joke. LOOK! I was about to have my head chopped off.

You try to come up with a better joke when you're under that kind of pressure.)

Despite the great joke, he looked at me blankly whilst scratching his beard.

'You have no idea what a tutor is do you?' I said.

'NO,' he bellowed. 'But I think you are making fun of me. GUARDS! Fetch me my biggest, sharpest, heaviest head-chopping axe.'

'Wait! I thought we were friends?' I squirmed.

'We are, but I miss chopping off heads. So, sorry and everything but I am the king and I get to do whatever I want, so there.'

I needed to act cool, relax, concentrate on the problem and work out how to solve it in a dignified manner. I turned my head as much as I could to face him, wriggled around so I was as close to his face as possible and said,

'AAARRRGGGGHHH!'

I don't think the king had had anyone scream, 'AAARRRGGGGHHH!' in his face before, because for a split second he released his grip on my collar and I dived into the musicians.

There was **chaos**. Musical instruments and musicians *flew* in all. *directions.* Harps, citoles, viols and hurdy-gurdys went everywhere and...

Woah! Wait! Pause the story a minute! I know we are right in the middle of a **VERY** exciting action-packed scene, but I have a question...

What is a hurdy-gurdy and who on earth chooses to play an instrument called a hurdy-gurdy?

(Apparently it's half-violin and half-piano.

Which is **super weird**. It's like sticking together half a flute and half a guitar and calling it a **fizzy-wizzy**, a jumbly-bumbly or a flutey-wooty. It's just silly is what it is! Also, playing a **hurdy-gurdy** is never going to impress anyone, is it?)

'I've written a song for you, it explains how I feel about you. I'll just go and get my **hurdy-gurdy**.'

'You look sad. I know how to cheer you up. Pass me that **hurdy-gurdy**.'

'Wait, we can't start the party, we don't have anyone to play the **hurdy-gurdy**.'

(Anyway, I've made my point, so let's get back to the action. I'll rewind a little and then carry on...)

There was **chaos**. Musical instruments and musicians *flew* in all. *directions*. Harps, citoles, viols and hurdy-gurdys went everywhere and in the **CONFUSION** I scrambled through the musical mess and caught my breath. I closed my eyes really tightly, held my breath for three seconds, quickly raised my right arm and pumped it UP and down really fast. I repeated the word 'home' over and over again. I heard King Henry let out a huge ROAR of anger but the noise was already starting to fade into the distance. I gave a huge sigh of relief. I was heading home.

CHAPTER 8

Mum was waiting outside the toilet when I opened the door. The amount of time I spend **TIME-TRAVELLING** doesn't matter, as I'm only ever gone a few minutes in the real world so Mum never has reason to question me.

'What have you got there?' (Uh-oh!)

'Where?'

'There, in your hand.'

I lifted my right hand and showed her it was empty.

'The other one,' she sighed, losing her patience.

I lifted my other hand. 'Oh, this?' I said, surprised to see that I was holding a weird small guitar-shaped instrument. 'It's a lute.'

'A what?' asked Mum.

'A lute.'

'What is a lute and why did you take it to the toilet?'

'Isn't it obvious?' I replied knowing that it wasn't at all obvious. I was just trying to buy myself some time until I could think of a good enough reason.

'Well, a lute is an ancient musical instrument popular in Tudor times and I was in the toilet... umm... learning to play it.'

'Why do you have a lute and where did you get it from?'

The truth was I must've grabbed it when I was trying to escape the king's clutches but I couldn't tell that to my mum, could I?

Answer: No

(Hmm, how would that go?)

Mum: Why do you have a lute and where did you get it from?

Me: I must've picked it up by mistake when I fell into the band when Henry VIII was trying to cut my head off.

Mum: Oh, OK, well have a nice day, dear.

UNLIKELY !!!

'Umm... it's just a craze at school at the moment you know? Last term it was fidget spinners, this term it's medieval string instruments.'

'And who gave you that one?'

'Henry.'

'Who's Henry? That's the first I've heard of anyone called Henry.'

'No, not Henry the first. I'm not sure he liked music. He was more interested in CONQUERING things.'

Mum stood there shaking her head in CONFUSION. She eventually gave up with me, shrugged her shoulders and went back into the kitchen. I walked back to my room without saying anything else. When I entered my room, my best friend, Ollie, was sitting on my bed reading a comic. He only lived around the corner and was always popping round.

'Hey,' he said.

'Hey,' I answered.

'Nice lute.' He nodded approvingly.

'You're so weird,' I told him.

'To be fair, I'm not the one who goes to the toilet with a string instrument popular in the Middle Ages.'

'Good point, well made.' I had no answer for that one.

Suddenly, my mum walked in to my bedroom with an armful of laundry.

'Ollie, are you part of this lute craze?' she asked.

'Lute craze?'

I used my best withering stare to fully influence his answer and make him say yes.

'No,' he said.

(NOTE TO SELF: continue to practise best withering stare.)

I was now standing behind my mum, looking directly at Ollie. I slowly mouthed the words 'SAY YES'. He caught my eye.

'Err... actually, yes... it's a HUGE craze really, the biggest. In fact, I've never seen a bigger craze in school.'

I signalled for him to stop. 'NO!' I mouthed. 'TOO MUCH!' He didn't see me.

'Everyone's walking around carrying lutes. Lutes, here, there and everywhere. You can't move for lutes in the corridor, lutes in the...'

Finally, Ollie noticed my frantic signalling.

'... but I prefer the hurdy-gurdy.'

'Do you indeed?' said Mum shaking her head in disbelief.

'How do you know what a hurdy-gurdy is?' I asked Ollie when my mum had left.

'Doesn't everyone?'

'No, literally no one our age knows what a hurdy-gurdy is. If anything, I'd say the word "hurdy", followed by "gurdy"

92

has never been used in a sentence uttered by anyone our age... ever.'

Ollie shrugged. 'How's the dancing coming along?' he asked, changing the subject.

'I think I have the basics but, I'm still not good enough to impress Chloe. I need to do more research.'

'My dad could teach you,' offered Ollie.

'Can he dance?'

'Nope.'

'Brilliant!' I slapped my hand to my forehead in exasperation. Sometimes Ollie was the smartest person I knew. Other times...

'This is a disaster. Chloe is going to go to the prom with Stu Hants Poo Pants, they'll be crowned prom king and queen and I'll wither away and disappear into nothing.' I sat on my bed and groaned.

'You could learn to moonwalk,' offered Ollie. 'You should look up **Neil Λrmstrong.**'

Hmmm, why would I look something up on the **INTERNET** when I can get all my information from the toilet? (Is another sentence that no one has ever said before.)

'That's a great idea! I'll be right back.' I stood to leave.

'Where are you going?'

'The **toilet.**'

'You've *just* been!' Ollie called after me, but I was already halfway down the hall.

I turned and locked the bathroom door. I jumped feet first into the bowl, flushed the chain and went through the **TIME-TRAVELLING** ritual. Down the bowl I shot, whirling, swirling, *this way*, that way, **up, down,** loud, quiet, etc., etc....

(Sorry, I'm not going to describe the entire

experience to you every time. Just go back a few pages if you want to know exactly what happens. It's OK. I'll wait...

...*whistling a tune*...

...

... OK, you're back. I'll continue...)

Everything suddenly went dark and really, really quiet. I was wearing... a spacesuit and a massive helmet. And it was a good job, as I was weightless, floating around in outer space. It was amazing! And then suddenly I was bouncing across the surface of the moon!

Right in front of me hovered another astronaut who I assumed, given the accuracy of my toilet travels thus far, was moonwalking Neil Armstrong.

'Hello!' I shouted, startling him. He

spun around (which sounds like he did it quickly but we were in **space,** remember, so with the moon's gravity it took ages... and **aaaages).** Finally he noticed me and looked shocked. Actually, he looked **HORRIFIED.** Imagine you were out with the cool kids from school and you were hanging out looking **COOL** and being **COOL** and you were totally **COOL** and then you turned around and your grandparents were standing there dressed like teenagers asking you to give them a big *smoochy kiss* to say hello – that's not even close to how **HORRIFIED** he looked.

'Errr... Houston, we have a problem.'

His voice was crackly and I realised I could hear him through small speakers in my helmet.

'Who's Houston and what's the problem?' I asked helpfully. 'Is Houston your *girlfriend?* Oooh! Are you having girlfriend problems? Me too. Although she isn't really my girlfriend... yet. She will be one day though, I'm sure, and we are definitely going to get married as long as she doesn't go to the prom with Stuart Hants and end up falling in love with his dance moves and marrying him.' I looked at Mr Armstrong but he just stared back at me.

I heard a loud buzz of static and then a distant voice in my helmet speaker.

'THIS IS HOUSTON. GO AHEAD. WHAT SEEMS TO BE THE PROBLEM?'

'There seems to be a young boy standing in front of me.'

Another blast of static.

'THIS IS HOUSTON. FOR A MINUTE THERE WE

97

THOUGHT YOU SAID THAT THERE WAS A YOUNG BOY ON THE MOON WITH YOU. PLEASE CONFIRM. OVER.'

'Affirmative, Houston. That is what I said. There is a young boy on the moon with me.'

'THIS IS HOUSTON. CAN YOU TELL US WHAT THIS "BOY" WANTS?'

'It seems he wants relationship advice,' said Neil.

'No! I don't!' I interrupted. 'Wait, maybe I do. Oh! I want to learn to dance.'

'Correction, Houston. It seems the boy wants to learn to dance.'

There was silence from the speakers. I hate long silences so I spoke. 'Wait! I'm CONFUSED,' I said.

'You're confused? Until a few seconds ago I thought I was the first man on the moon. Now I find out a boy has followed me up here hoping I'll give him dance lessons so he can go to the prom. What are you doing here?'

'Ollie said I should—'

'Ollie?'

'My best friend.'

'Is he here too?' Neil asked.

'No, he doesn't know how to use the toilet.'

'What?'

'Nothing. Look, he's in my bedroom waiting for me to get back. Anyway, he said I needed to learn to moonwalk and you are on the moon and... hang on... moonwalking is a dance, but someone and something is wrong in this situation. You aren't a dancer by any chance are you?'

'I'm Neil Armstrong. The astronaut. The first man on the moon.'

'Hmmm, you couldn't show me how to

moonwalk could you?'

'Sure, things couldn't get any weirder.'

And with that Mr Armstrong bounced off across the surface of the moon shouting, 'Hippity-hoppity, hippity-hoppity'.

(Note to reader: look it up, he actually really did say this.)

It looked fun but it wasn't a very good dance.

'I'm not sure Ollie knew what he was talking about when... By the way, what year are we?'

'1969.'

'Hmm... I think I need to get back home.'

'Well, you can wait here, I'm sure a bus will be along shortly.'

'I didn't know that there were buses on the moon—'

'OF COURSE THERE AREN'T

BUSES! THIS IS THE MOON!'

he shouted.

'Oh right, yes, of course. You're trying to be **funny** and *ANGRY* at the same time.'

'I think the lack of atmosphere may be getting to me. I need to lie down. I think I'm going crazy,' Neil muttered to himself.

'If you are going *mad,* and you are on the *moon* then you might be a lunar-tic!' I joked.

(Nothing. He just stared at me.)

'A lunar-tic,' I repeated.

(More blank staring.)

'Because lunar is another word for the moon and a lunatic is a—'

Suddenly Neil jumped in the air and bounced away from me shouting, *'Hippity-hoppity, hippity-hoppity'.* I tried to follow but

I couldn't move very well in my **spacesuit**
and didn't get very far.

Neil laughed at my attempt. **'That's one
small step! You should take a giant leap...'**
And off he hopped, giggling to himself.

I had **no idea** what he was on about,
but it was clearly time to leave. I said the
words and performed the actions that would
take me home, I took one last look around the
moon and leaped into the air. As I did so
I vanished from **1969** and ended up back
safely on Earth in the present day.

I ran back into my room. (Remember, time
stands still in the real world, so to Ollie it
seemed I had run into the bathroom and straight
back out again.)

'Ollie, why did you say I had to look up **Neil
Armstrong?** He can't dance, he was the
first man to land on the **moon.**'

Ollie thought for a few moments. 'No, wait! Wrong moonwalk, sorry! Not **Neil Armstrong**. I didn't mean him. Wait, what's that?' he asked, pointing at me.

I looked down and realised I was still holding my astronaut's helmet. 'Oh, this? It's a spaceman's helmet,' I said matter-of-factly. 'For my moonwalking.'

Ollie laughed out loud. 'That's funny!' He screamed. 'You do know moonwalking is a *dance*, right?'

'Of course.' I laughed awkwardly. 'Well, I do now,' I thought.

I had learned a valuable lesson. I should always *research* where I'm going **BEFORE** heading there.

I went online and looked up moonwalking. The dance was a move whereby you slid your feet along so it looked like you were going *forwards* when actually you are going **backwards**. I decided not to learn it as, if I tried it when I was dancing with *Chloe*, I'd probably end up sliding out the front door and end up in the car park, and then Stu Hants **Poo** Pants would rush in and finish the dance with Chloe.

'There's always **ELVIS PRESLEY.** You could learn some moves from the king of **rock 'n' roll.'**

The king of rock 'n' roll, eh? I thought. A **KING** that is more likely to dance than chop my head off. That sounds like the kind of king that I'd like to meet.

As soon as Ollie went home, I did my research into **ELVIS PRESLEY** and found out:

1. He was considered very **COOL.**

2. He was in the American Army. I tried

to find out what rank he was but the computer said 'PRIVATE', so, I didn't like to ask.

3. (Number 2 was an excellent joke. Well done me.)

4. Ladies absolutely *loved* him, especially when he danced. This is very good news. I don't need lots of ladies to like me, just one. Chloe Onions. (You didn't need me to tell you that though, did you? I mean, if you got to this point in the book and thought **'who is he talking about?'** then you really haven't been paying attention at all and I suggest you go back to the start.)

5. Apparently **ELVIS** died on the toilet. I need to meet this guy. We have so much in common. I don't mean I died

on the toilet – nor do I plan to, for that matter – but we both have a **toilet** that features heavily in our life stories. A fellow toileteer.

Is that a thing? A toileteer? At first I thought it sounded like an ***ADVENTURER,*** but on second thoughts, it sounds like something you should go and see a doctor about.

Doctor: Hello, what seems to be the problem?

Me: Hello, Doctor, I have toileteer.

Doctor: I've not heard of toileteer. Do you mean you have a toilet-shaped ear or you go to the toilet from your ear? Or someone else has gone to the toilet in your ear?

(Something like that, anyway. Where was I?)

'Right then,' I thought to myself, I guess I'm going back in history to track down the king of **rock 'n' roll, MR ELVIS PRESLEY,** to learn how to dance like a professional.

CHAPTER 9

The following day was an **interesting** one.
For a start, I had chicken legs.

Not literally! Come on!! That would be ridiculous! I mean, _**be serious.**_ If I woke up and tried to get out of bed only to find that my legs had been replaced with chicken legs then I don't think I'd describe the day to you as "interesting".

Terrible? Yes!

Shocking? Absolutely!

Worrying? Totally!

Completely and utterly terrifying? 100%!

But not *interesting*.

Anyway, chicken was for dinner. Before that, I had school lunch to deal with.

When I got to the front of the line the dinner lady **GROWLED** at me. She was short with crazy hair and never, ever smiled at anyone. I tried to be polite and cheerful.

'Hello, Miss. What's for lunch today?'

'Drumsticks.'

'Chicken?'

'Wood.'

'Have you deep-fried actual drum sticks?' I asked but she just shrugged.

'I'll have a sandwich.'

So, I was just finishing my sandwich, when I saw my future girlfriend Chloe Onions.

She looked *beautiful* AND she was looking my way AND smiling AND... Wait... she was waving. Quick Ted wave back!

I raised my hand to wave back, only to be **rudely** barged out of the way by her best friend, Sandra Wum (also known as **Sandy Bum**).

'Oi!' I shouted a bit too loudly. The dinner hall went quiet.

'What is your problem?' snapped Sandra.

Quick, Ted, think of something cool to say to put her in her place and let her know that I, Ted Jones, won't be pushed out of the way by anyone!

'I'm not a window, you know'. Yes, you read that correctly, I just announced to the whole school that I wasn't a window.

'Huh?' said Sandra.

'I mean, I'm not SEE-THROUGH...
you know... like a window...' I explained a lot
quieter and more sheepishly than before.

'Oh, OK, like, sure,' she said shrugging.
'Thanks for, like, letting me know that you
aren't a window!' The whole hall
erupted in laughter.

I blushed.

When the laughter finally died down,
Martin Harris, the school
bully, suddenly shouted out, 'Hey! I've just
farted. Someone open Ted!'
And the laughter started again. I sat back
at my lunch table feeling totally
embarrassed.

'Don't worry,' said Ollie. ' I knew what you
meant.'

'Really? You did?' I asked hopefully.

'*Absolutely,* kind of... well, maybe... or... no,

111

not really, I mean you told **Sandra** that you weren't a window. I agree, you aren't a window. But I'm still Confused as to why you didn't say you weren't a fridge or a chair or a **carrot?'**

'Would that have been any better?'

'Not really, nO. I was just wondering, that's all.'

'Well, don't.'

'OK,' Ollie agreed. 'Oh, by the way...'

'What?' I asked, thinking things couldn't get any worse today.

'Stuart Hants is heading over towards Chloe. He might be about to ask her to the prom. Quick, I'll stall him, you get to Chloe first.'

Ollie ran off to stop Stuart. This was it, my moment, but I wasn't ready. My moment had come to me at the wrong moment, but I couldn't let my moment become Stu Pants **Poo** Pants's moment. But, I still couldn't dance very well. I knew a bit more than I did a few days ago but not **_nearly_** enough to impress Chloe. Oh well, I still have time to learn. First things first, ask Chloe to go to the prom with me. Here goes.

I **_RUSHED_** over to Chloe, who was deep in conversation with Sandra, and I interrupted them.

"**Hey,**" I said.

'Hey,' she said.

(Great start. It was going well.)

'Oh, by the way, Chloe, **Ted** isn't a window. In case you, like, thought he was a window. He, like, told me just before,' whispered **Sandra,** trying to be funny. She looked at me and laughed before folding her arms and walking off to **annoy** someone else.

'I... umm... so I guess you heard the whole... umm... window thing...'

'I did,' she smiled.

'Err... yeah... sorry about that...' I stuttered.

'Is it just windows you have an issue with or is it doors and air conditioning units too?' Chloe smiled.

'No, just windows,' I smiled. 'Although I'm not a sliding patio door either. It's important you know that too.'

'You are so weird, Ted Jones,' she giggled. 'And I think you might be getting stranger every day.'

'I know, I'm sorry, but... umm... I wanted to ask you something... Would you want to umm... you know... if you aren't... I thought maybe we... I mean you and I... at the... umm...' I stuttered, unable to get the right words out.

'Are you trying to ask me to go to the prom with you?'

'Umm... I... errr...' I blushed.

'Will you go to the prom with me?'

There, I said it...

Wait! That didn't come from my mouth. It came from Stu Hants **Poo** Pants who was standing next to me, grinning his stupidest grin at **Chloe.** I'd become shy and **nervous** and I'd failed to say the right words at the right time and now Stupid Stu (ooh, that's good, I should remember that one for later!) asked her before me. **Noooooooo!!!**

'Oh, I'm sorry, Stuart. I can't, I'm already going with **Ted.**'

'I understand,' I said. 'Well, never mind I hope you both enjoy the... **WAIT!**

WHAT? Did you just say...?'

No way! Chloe chose me! Over stupid Stu Hants **Poo** Pants with his **BIG** stupid pants of **poo.**

I have a date for the prom!

(And a new nickname for Stuart Hants.)

I have a **DATE** for the prom!

(And a new nickname for Stuart Hants.)

I have a DATE for the prom!

(And a new nickname for Stuart Hants.)

'Cool,' I said, trying to look cool but inwardly **shaking** like a chocolate mousse on a rollercoaster. Luckily I'd kept my composure perfectly and she hadn't noticed.

'Cool,' replied Chloe, smiling at me.

'Good,' I said.

'Yep.' She nodded, *still* smiling. 'Shall we

talk about this another time when you aren't shaking so much?'

'Oh, umm... yeah. That'd be better. It's... ummm, really cold in here. **BRRR.**' I blushed – and when I say blushed, I mean I went **bright red.** My face was so red that three cars pulled up alongside me and waited for my face to go green before driving off.

(Hahaha, that's quite funny.)

(Well done me!)

'I'll see you later, Ted,' she sang and skipped off down the corridor.

I am so happy!

I am so SCARED!

I need the toilet!

(For a few different reasons.)

CHAPTER 10

When I got home from school I **RAN** up to my room, powered up my computer and did some more research into **ELVIS PRESLEY.** Ollie was right about one thing: **rock 'n' roll** music was **good.** **ELVIS'S** first single was released in 1956 and it was called 'HEARTBREAK HOTEL'. That's where I'll be checking into if I embarrass myself on the dance floor in front of Chloe. (Sigh.)

I turned up the volume and tried wiggling

my hips like **ELVIS**, but it just looked like I was trying to dislodge a wedgie from my bum. I opted for shuffling **backwards** and *forwards* and throwing my arms around like I was being attacked by a wasp. I caught my moves in my bedroom mirror and sighed. I was an **AWFUL** dancer. I had no rhythm. I went back to studying **ELVIS** on the internet. I listened to more of his songs: I Can't Stop Loving You, I'm So Lonesome I Could Cry, Can't Help Falling In Love. **ELVIS** is describing my relationship with Chloe. He totally gets me. I have to meet him but at what point in his career?

I kept watching his videos and looking through his life story and then I spotted the perfect time and place to travel back to.

On 14th January 1973, **ELVIS** performed the first ever concert by a solo artist that was broadcast around the world on TV. It was apparently watched in **40** countries by 1.5 billion people!

1.5 BILLION PEOPLE!

More people than watched the moon landing!

More people than when I announced to **Sandra Wum** that I wasn't a window.

Here's what else I found out about it:

- He didn't charge any money for the tickets. Instead, people were asked to pay whatever they wanted and all the money went to charity.
- The concert was held at the Honolulu International Centre in **Hawaii**, a beautiful, tropical island in the Pacific Ocean.

- I've not been to **Hawaii**.
- I want to go to **Hawaii**.
- I'm going to **Hawaii**.
- **Hawaii. Hawaii. Hawaii**.

I went into the toilet and took my shoes off like always. Just as I pulled my second sock off, **Mum burst in** – Oh no! I'd forgotten to lock the door!

'**OH!** What are you doing in here?'

'Going to the toilet.'

'Why are you taking your socks off?'

'They're wet,' I answered, too quickly.

'Wet? Did you do a peepee in your trousers?'

'**WHAT!** No I didn't do a peepee in my trousers! I didn't mean my socks were wet, I meant they... **smell.**'

121

'Smell?'

'Yes, I have really smelly feet.'

'Give me them,' she said, taking my socks and holding them to her nose and breathing in a little too enthusiastically.

'They smell *lovely*.'

'You're so weird, Mum.'

'Fine, I'll give them a wash. Hurry up in the toilet, I need to go,' said Mum before turning and walking out, closing the door behind her.

I quickly **LOCKED IT,** climbed into the toilet and flushed the chain. I heard Mum calling, 'I mean it! Don't be too looooooooong.' Her voice faded as I spun round and round and disappeared down the U-bend.

After a few moments, I noticed the lights around me were becoming **brighter** and more colourful. There were red, green

and blue bursts of colour slowly pulsating –
like a disco! I took this as a good sign. I shut
my eyes and relaxed.

Suddenly I heard a **loud** commotion.
I opened my eyes and looked around. I found
myself in a narrow corridor. It was full of
people **RUSHING** *this* way and **that**.
Everyone seemed to be in a great hurry.
I saw two men standing next to a large
speaker. I went up to them.

'Excuse me? Where exactly are we
right now?'

The two men looked confused. One of
them spoke. **'Hawaii.'**

'I'm fine, thank you,' I answered. 'But
where exactly are we right now?' The
two men shook their heads and continued
pushing the speaker up the corridor.
A woman **RUSHED** past me whilst

YELLING into a microphone attached to a pair of headphones. I avoided her and stepped backwards as a man carrying a keyboard nearly bumped into me. I apologised and stepped out of his way and nearly **COLLIDED** with two women pushing a clothes rail full of shiny sequined outfits. I needed to find a safe place to stand, out of the way of these busy people, I thought to myself. The woman with the clipboard **HURRIED** back the other way shouting orders into her microphone. As she passed by, a piece of paper dropped from her clipboard. I picked it up and read the title.

ELVIS PRESLEY
Aloha from Hawaii
14th January 1973

Yes! I was in the right time and place.

I saw a gap in the traffic and darted into a doorway. The door was ajar and I peeked in. Inside was a brightly lit room full of empty chairs. **Rock 'n' roll** music was blaring out of two huge speakers. A large video camera on a tripod with wheels spun around filming the action and on the far side was a stage with a group of backing dancers on. Behind them were huge red letters that lit up and spelled out the name **ELVIS.** Abruptly the music stopped and a voice came over the speakers.

'OK, that was a **good rehearsal** but let's go again from the top please. First positions, everyone.'

I moved through the door a little so I could get a good view and suddenly saw someone I recognised. He had his hair brushed forward in a **HUGE QUIFF**, like a squirrel's tail but **COOLER** (although having hair like a squirrel's tail is pretty cool, I imagine).

He was wearing sunglasses and the most incredible all-in-one jumpsuit. It was white with gold and diamonds all over it. Around his neck he wore a lei (a necklace of multicoloured flowers). He turned round and I gasped as I caught sight of a gold American Eagle on the back of his suit. He looked awesome!

I stood and watched him rehearse. His dance moves were amazing.

He swayed his hips to the LEFT.

(I could do that.)

He swayed his hips to the RIGHT.

(I could do that.)

He thrust his hips **backwards** and **forwards**.

(I could do that – but I'm not going to.)

He **WOBBLED** his legs like they were made of rubber. (I could do that too.)

And he karate kicked around the stage.

(In my head I think I can do that but in reality I might look like a dog trying to wee up against a tree.)

What I'm **trying** to say is that I could do most of these moves. They weren't complicated they were just in the right order and in time with the music. I watched the dancing from the doorway and tried to copy some of the moves until suddenly the music stopped.

'Thank you, **MR PRESLEY.** Backing dancers, stay where you are please!' shouted a voice from somewhere in the darkness. Everyone on the stage jostled

127

to find their starting position as **ELVIS** stepped down from the stage and headed straight over to where I was standing. This was my opportunity. I had to speak to him. I stepped out from where I was ducking down watching the performance.

'Hello, **MR PRESLEY**, sir,' I said, offering my hand to shake. He shook it, whipped off his sunglasses and smiled.

'Hey, what's happening, kid? What can I do for you?' he said.

(Actually, with his accent and the way he spoke so fast, it sounded more like, **'Heywhat's-happeningkidwhatcanIdoforyou?'**)

'I'm going to prom with a girl who I really, really want to impress but I don't know how to dance properly. Can you give me any tips at all? Anything? Please!' I blurted out.

'Well now,' he said with a chuckle. 'What you want to do is just *feel* the music, **uh-huh,** you know what I'm saying? Let the music take control and just *feeeeeeel* it.' **ELVIS** rocked his hips, wobbled his legs and swung his arm like a windmill. 'You understand me now? *Feeeeeeeel* it.'

'So I should *feeeeeeeeel* it?' I replied.

'**Uh-huh,** that's right, kid, you gotta *feeeeeeel* it. Aint no good if you don't *feeeeeeeeel* it. You got what I'm saying now, kid?'

'I think so, **MR PRESELY**.'

'Well now, good luck with the lucky lady, kid.' And with that he put his sunglasses back on and walked off down the corridor.

I stood there for a few moments. I'd just met **rock 'n' roll** royalty and he was **awesome!**

Suddenly, I jumped in surprise as the music started up again. The background dancers began to dance a routine of twists and turns and handclaps all perfectly timed with the beat of the music. As I watched I started to copy the moves. Left, right, swing your hips, clap, turn. This was it! I was *feeeeeeeeeling* it.

I WAS **DANCING!**

After a few minutes I was totally nailing it. I could *feeeeeeel* it all over. I was even keeping time... kind of. Suddenly I felt a hand on my shoulder. I spun round and there was a large, *STERN-LOOKING* woman standing over me.

'All dancers need to be in costume by now. We are running late. Quickly, follow me to room five and hurry up and get changed.' She snapped, turning on her heel and marching off.

I did what I was told and immediately followed her. What could possibly go wrong?

BONG! BONG!

CHAPTER 11

Everything went wrong.

I followed the lady down the corridor.

'Come on, you really need to get a move on. We can't run late today.'

I was ever so slightly starting to **panic**.

'I don't want to hold anyone up. I need to get changed like all the other dancers...'

Hang on...

WHAT?

She thinks that because I was...

132

... and the *feeeeeling* it...

... and now she **. . . !**

I'm not a dancer.

I can't dance!

Uh oh! This is bad.

'Another one for you,' barked the woman.

'Make this one **QUICK**, we're running late!'

Another woman grabbed my arm and guided me into a chair. She whipped a sheet around me and tied it at the neck.

'I... umm...' I stuttered.

'**SHHH!** No time to talk. You're late. The audience have started to arrive,' she **SNAPPED.** So I sat there for what seemed like ages while she flitted around me with various *brushes, powders, glitters* and *gels*. This was the first time I'd had make-up on. I checked the mirror and... well... I looked quite good!

The make-up artist took a step back, checked my face and whipped the sheet off. 'Have you got **bell bottoms?**'

'Well that's a bit personal isn't it? I'm quite happy with the current shape of my bottom thank you very much,' I told her.

'They are a type of trouser where the end **flares** out. How do you not know that?' she asked shaking her head suspiciously. 'Just put this on quickly,' she sighed, grabbing a sparkly one-piece outfit from a clothes rail and handing it to me.

'Get dressed, now!'

I didn't want to argue (and I really wanted to see what I looked like in a sparkly jumpsuit just like **ELVIS!**).

I turned to the make-up artist. 'Excuse me?' I said. 'Where are the changing rooms?'

She looked at me like I was **completely** mad, 'This isn't a shopping mall, *darling*,' she laughed. 'Just get changed here and quickly. You are a dancer, **aren't you?**'

'Of course!' I lied. 'Right, no peeking.'

I quickly changed into the jumpsuit. I turned to look at myself in the large mirror.

'No time for that, sweetie. Get to the stage. Now!' she shouted.

I **RAN OFF** down the corridor and skidded round the corner, through the doorway and onto the stage ready to perform as a dancer.

And then I remembered.

I'M NOT A DANCER!

What on earth am I doing?

I, Terry Barry Larry Gary Harry Jerry Perry Lenny Benny Johnny Tommy Julie Jones, am about to perform on **live television.**

'Stand by, everyone! Make sure you are perfect.'

I turned to the dancer next to me. She was also wearing a sparkly all-in-one jumpsuit just like mine.

'Quickly,' I whispered to her. 'I've forgotten how to dance. What do I do?'

'What?' she hissed back. 'You're just **nervous.** Relax. Listen to the music and do **whatever** you want.'

'Really?' I asked hopefully.

'NO OF COURSE NOT! We've rehearsed this for SIX months. Do **_exactly_** what you were taught and don't take a single step wrong. They are expecting over a **_billion_** people to tune in.'

A billion what now?!?!

No, no, no, no. I can't have a

BILLION people see me dance. In the past I have performed to exactly... umm... hang on... let me just work it out... umm... wait a minute... just working out the final number... (add 2, carry 3... minus 1...)

NO ONE!!

No one has EVER seen me dance. Because I CAN'T dance!

'We are live in 5...'

'No, no, no!'

'... 4...'

Wait, wait, wait! I can't do this. Suddenly the lights all came on, the big red letters that spelled ELVIS lit up, 18,000 people in the audience jumped to their feet and started screaming, red lights appeared on the top of the cameras, the music started up and the other dancers started to *sway*. I **swayed** too and immediately noticed that I was going **left** to *right* when everyone else was going *right* to **left!** I tried to correct myself and knocked into the lady next to me who glared at me through a fake smile.

'... **3**...'

Oh no! Oh no, no, no!

'What are you doing?'

I heard a voice from the side of the stage and turned to see the lady with the headphones and the clipboard that I'd seen earlier. 'Get off the stage. NOW! Before anyone notices.'

Uh oh. She looked super ANGRY.

Time to go!

I pumped my arm up and down and said the words to take me home.

'... **2**... and **1**... WE ARE LIVE.'

But I was already heading home.

Wow, that was close! The biggest live televised performance of the 1910s and I was just seconds away from completely ruining it!

I arrived back home, climbed out of the toilet, unlocked the door and RUSHED straight into my mum who was still standing outside, crossing her legs.

'Come on, come on, I'm about to wet myself!' she shouted, trying to elbow me out of the way.

'MUM! Too much information!' I shook my head in disgust.

Mums should not talk about such things.

In fact there are lots of things mums shouldn't talk about.

I've made a list:

Things mums **SHOULD NOT talk about... EVER!**

- Wetting their pants for *any* reason (including laughing really hard).

- How handsome certain men who they see on the telly are *especially* if they say they want to snog them. (GROSS!)

- Things that are cool. (They immediately stop being cool the moment your mum thinks they are cool.)

'Hang on a minute!' shrieked Mum. 'What have you done to your face?' I turned around to check my reflection in the bathroom mirror and gasped. I was still covered in glitter and make-up.

'I was... ummm... experimenting...'

'With my expensive make-up?'

'No.'

'Well it's not your father's, is it? Wait a minute, it's not your father's, is it?'

'No. Of course not. I was just experimenting with a GLAM look for the prom.'

'Right, well... whatever, I need a wee. Move.' And she pushed past me and shut the door.

I went back into my bedroom, where Ollie was sitting on the floor, flicking through a book.

'When did you...? Never mind.'

Ollie just shrugged.

'I think I know how to dance now,' I told him.

'What? You've only been in the toilet for *three minutes!*' he replied without looking up.

(So that's when he arrived.)

141

'Well, I used the time wisely.'

'What? Bearing in mind it takes about 60 seconds to do a **number one** and a few minutes to do a **number two...**

(I once ate a dodgy fish stew and think I did a number 37!)

'...Taking into account the time spent for trouser and underpants arrangements that leaves approximately **45** seconds in which you are now telling me you learned how to dance.'

'Correct!'

(He **clearly** hadn't noticed I had a face full of MAKE-UP.)

'And at what point did you have time to do your MAKE-UP?"

(Oh, he had noticed.)

'There was enough time... just.'

'Oh, OK.' Ollie will literally believe anything I say. 'And you are **totally confident** that you are now able to dance well enough and have nailed the right look to impress Chloe and the rest of the school? That's **everyone** in the **whole school** judging you and your dance ability and your make-up application skills which you say you perfected in 45 seconds whilst standing or sitting in the toilet either pre- or post-**toilet-y** things.'

'Correct,' I said, nodding my head confidently.

'Well, you don't look confident. **Sparkly,** yes, but confident, **no.**'

As you can see, Ollie was not being terribly encouraging.

'Not even with my confident head nod?'
I was doing a very specific type of head
nod to indicate confidence. I even threw
in a fancy hand movement and then spun
on my heel. It would've looked **SO COOL**
had I not knocked over my bedside light,
become tangled in the cord and ended up
falling flat on my face.

'Oh yes, no sorry, that was totally cool,'
scoffed Ollie, staring at me as I tried to
untangle myself.

'Well, OK, it needs a little work but I'm
nearly there. Right, time you went
home so I can practise.'

'I'd go a little lighter on the lipstick and
glittery eyes,' he suggested.

'Noted,' I replied.

Ollie gathered up his things and left,
leaving me wondering how on earth I'm going

to be ready to impress the whole school and be so awesome that I bring tears to *Chloe Onions's* eyes.

DID YOU JUST LAUGH?

LOOK! I've told you before, **I GET IT!** Onions make you cry! That doesn't mean you *laugh* every time I put 'crying' and 'onions' in the same sentence. **IT'S NOT FUNNY!** Now, go and think about your behaviour while I practise my dancing and remove my **MAKE-UP.**

CHAPTER 12

Wait! Before I tell you what happened at the prom, I think we should take a break. A lot has happened to me recently and so it feels like the perfect time to give you another chance to ask me any questions that you might have. If you have a question, send it to tedstoilet@mail.com. OK, go ahead, ask me anything.

Your question: Do you think you and Chloe will ever become boyfriend and girlfriend?

My answer: I don't know. I'm not a mind reader, am I? If I was, this book wouldn't be called Ted & his Time-Travelling Toilet it would be called Martin & His Mind-Reading Motorbike.

(Note to self: Write a best-selling series of books entitled Martin & His Mind-Reading Motorbike.)

However, I will say that as soon as Chloe realises that I am the most handsome, clever, talented, funniest person in the school then yes, she will definitely want to be my girlfriend.

Your question: You said earlier in this book that if, just before you start your adventure, you suddenly need the toilet, then you can just go. This seems a little... unhygienic.

My answer: Umm, OK, you are right, it does sound a little... gross. If the situation arose, I'd probably go, leave it a while, then go back in and time-travel. I wouldn't want there to be a hold-up somewhere and end up bumping into something horrible.

Your question: Can dogs whistle?

My answer: ARE YOU SERIOUS? I have the only time-travelling toilet in the whole entire world. I can travel through thousands of years of history and meet anyone who has ever existed and ask them anything and yet the only question that you can think of asking me

– the only question you actually want me to answer – is 'can dogs whistle?' UNBELIEVABLE! NEXT QUESTION!

Your question: I am considering learning to play the hurdy-gurdy and I—
My answer: Right, that's it, the break is over. No more questions. Back to the story.

There was lots of excitement in the air the morning of the prom. We still had to have lessons all day because my school is nice like that, but none of the students were paying attention.

Miss Makeshift was trying to get us to sit down and concentrate which was like asking a monkey in a zoo to not throw his poop at the zookeeper! No one was listening to her. They were more concerned about what they were going to wear, how they were going to dance, what they were going to eat, etc., etc. Every time a vehicle pulled into the school car park, everyone **RAN OVER TO THE WINDOW** to watch something exciting (like a chair or a table) get delivered. Miss Makeshift was having problems keeping control.

'Please sit down, class. It's only a *table*.'

'Two tables, Miss,' shouted Josh.

'It doesn't matter. The only tables I want you to concentrate on are your TIMES TABLES. Now settle down or none of you will be going to the prom.' She folded her arms and tried to look cross but we all knew that no teacher on earth could be that **mean.**

Eventually she gave up and just seemed to stare into space and dream of being anywhere other than with us.

During break, Ollie caught up with me.

'How's the dance practice going?'

'Good,' I answered with confidence.

'Great, because I wouldn't want you to embarrass yourself in front of the entire school, as a mistake like that will never ever be forgotten and you will *always* be known as 'the boy who thought he could dance but couldn't', and then Chloe definitely wouldn't want to date you. Even **Awful Annie** wouldn't want to date you and the rumour is that she once dated a boy who looked like the Gruffalo... Just saying.'

'Thank you, Ollie. You have made me feel *so much less nervous* than I was two minutes ago,' I hissed.

I had a weird feeling in my tummy. It was churning around and around like a washing machine. Mum once told me it was called having butterflies but I don't believe her as I have never knowingly eaten a butterfly.

I once ate a fly.

It flew into my mouth when I yawned and I swallowed it by mistake. Mum said it wouldn't hurt me but everyone knows that flies eat poo* and so eating one can't be a good thing.

(*Why do flies eat poo? Why don't they go to nice restaurants, like people?)

(See the opposite page for a restaurant menu for posh flies.)

THE FLY-VY

MENU FOR FLIES

STARTERS

Crispy POOdle salad

DUMPlings

MAINS

BOTroast

FARTuccine

HaliBUTT

Egg Fu DUNG

All main courses are served with

POOtatoes and Pees

DESSERTS

Apple BUMble

Eton 'Dog' Mess

I couldn't concentrate for the rest of the day. All I kept thinking about is that I have an opportunity to impress the best-looking girl in the school and I might **MESS IT UP** because I'm not sure I'm ready. In the past, I'd return back from **TIME-TRAVELLING** and I'd be full of confidence, but this was different.

Finally, the bell to signal the end of the day rang. My class cheered. I expected the teacher, Mr Marks, to tell us off but he had given up by then and looked pleased to see us leave. Everyone *RAN OUT OF THE SCHOOL* excitedly. I was just walking up to the gates when *Chloe* caught up with me.

'So, what time will I see you later?' she asked.

'My mum said she would take us so, about seven?'

'OK.' She smiled. 'Have you got your dancing shoes ready? I really want us to be crowned prom king and queen,' she giggled.

'Ah! I don't have specific dancing shoes just... umm... shoes really.'

Chloe laughed. 'It's just a figure of speech. I didn't expect you to *actually* have dancing shoes. But you can dance... can't you?'

'Me? Of course. I've had lessons.'

'Really? Cool. Who from?'

I decided not to tell her that my teachers were Henry VIII and ELVIS PRESLEY, in case she thought I was even weirder than she currently thinks I am.

'Henry VIII and ELVIS PRESLEY.' I blurted out.

'You are so weird, Ted,' she laughed.

(One day I'll master the art of not saying

out loud what I'm thinking.)

'See you later, Ted,' Chloe called out as she climbed into her parents' car and slammed the door. I waited and watched as they drove off.

I felt sick. Maybe I'm not well. I should call her when I get home and tell her I can't go to the prom because I'm too ill.

No, Come on, Ted! You'll be fine. Go home, practise your dancing one more time and everything will be OK. You've got this.

CHAPTER 13

'You're very quiet. Are you OK?' asked my mum as we drove home.

'Yes, I'm fine,' I sighed.

'You don't look well. As soon as we get home, I'll put the kettle on.'

'I'm not ill and I don't want a cup of tea, thank you. I'm just nervous.'

'Awww...it's your first prom, dressing up smart, taking a young lady. It's all part of growing up.'

'Yes, yes, I know but I don't want to

make a fool of myself. You know, dancing.'

'But when you were younger you were a FABULOUS dancer.'

'Mum! I used to bob up and down on my toes and then skip round and round the dance floor. I'm unlikely to win a dancing reality TV show with those moves, am I?'

'Oh, I don't know. Your grandma used to love watching you dance.'

'Well, it's a shame she isn't judging prom king and queen then, isn't it?'

'I could give her a call and ask her. The old people's home would like to take her out for a few hours.'

'NO! NO! NO! NO! NO!'

My mum's car pulled into our driveway and she opened up the house and let me in. I RAN UPSTAIRS taking off my hat, coat, shoes, socks and jumper and dropping them all the way up the stairs as I usually did. Mum followed me up, gathering the items of clothing that I'd shed.

'I've got a surprise for you,' she called out to me from her bedroom.

'What is it? You aren't considering moving house or changing the bathroom again are you?' I called back, rummaging through my wardrobe looking for something smart to wear for the prom that didn't contain stains.

'No, no, your father thought it was all too expensive so it's all on hold for the time being,' she sighed. 'But, look,' she said walking into my room with an armful of clothes wrapped carefully in cellophane.

'What are they?'

'Suits. I went to the store and hired you

something to wear tonight.'

'WOW!' I said looking at the royal blue suit jacket. 'It's amazing.'

'Do you like the blue one? I couldn't decide so I hired you a black one too.'

'No, this is—'

'...and a white one, and a cream coloured one and this one is like a dark red, and this one is more of a—'

'Blue is perfect, Mum. I love the blue one. It fits perfectly.' I interrupted, holding it up and admiring myself in the mirror.'

'Wait, I haven't got a—'

'Shirt? I have one here, and a tie and I've polished your smart shoes.'

'You are the BEST, Mum!' I beamed. 'Thank you so much, I'm going to look amazing.'

With renewed confidence I spent the next

few hours practising the moves that **Henry VIII** and **ELVIS** had taught me. I had the radio blaring and I tried **NEW MOVES** every time a new song started playing. Eventually I turned off the music and started getting changed.

When I was dressed I looked in the mirror and smiled. *I looked good,* even if I say so myself. I sneaked into my dad's room and rubbed on a *splash* of his aftershave.

It smelled awful!

At that moment, Mum wandered in to check on me.

'Dad's aftershave is **horrible.** It smells of mint.'

'That's mouthwash, Ted. The aftershave bottle is next to it.'

'AARRRGGHH!'

'It's fine, just wash it off and rub this on.'
She handed me a small bottle with *French*
writing on and I sprayed it on my neck. It
smelled a lot better than the mouthwash.

'Right, are you ready? Let's go and pick up
your prom date.'

I took a deep breath and *smiled nervously*. 'Yep, let's go.'

We drove the short distance to Chloe's
house. Mum talked non-stop but I was too
distracted to reply. She didn't seem to mind.
When we pulled up outside Chloe's, I got
out of the car and walked up her garden
path. I took a moment to compose myself
and then **rang the doorbell**.
Chloe eventually opened the door. She was
wearing a red, sparkly dress. I'd never
seen her wear anything other than school
uniform. She looked INCREDIBLE!

'You look lovely,' I smiled.

'So do you, Ted,' she replied.

I blushed. Why was I blushing? I was **so nervous** my emotions were all over the place. Chloe waved goodbye to her parents and we made our way back to my mum's car. Mum was *grinning* from ear to ear.

'**Stop** *smiling,*' I hissed. 'You look **creepy.**'

'I can't help it, you are so sweet together.'

'Stop it! **Don't** say anything to **embarrass me. Please!**' I begged, but before she could answer, Chloe climbed into the car and put her seat belt on.

'Hello, Mrs Jones,' she *giggled.*

'Nice to meet you, Chloe. You look lovely,' *smiled* Mum.

There was a little too much *smiling* for

my liking. I mean, yes, it was an exciting thing we were doing and we were all dressed up, but there was no need for so much *smiling* was there?

Conversation was awkward and limited in the car with Mum asking typical boring mum questions like, **'Did you have a nice day at school?'** and **'What subjects do you like?'** and *YAWN* I'm even boring myself repeating the questions to you now. The journey seemed to take forever but was actually only less than ten minutes.

I JUMPED OUT as soon as the car was parked, and said goodbye to Mum. I walked with Chloe through the school gates. I'd like to have held her hand but I wasn't that brave. I mean I **TRAVEL BACK IN TIME** and nearly had to fight off Henry VIII (which is pretty brave) but holding a girl's hand in public? **NO WAY!**

The playground was *packed* with kids in suits and dresses, *giggling* and **LAUGHING.** We walked across the playground to the hall and stepped through the large glass doors. The school hall looked *amazing!* There was an arch of multi-coloured *balloons* in the doorway. In the far corner was a **DJ** surrounded by an array of **DISCO LIGHTS.** There was a huge glitter ball dangling from the ceiling, filling the room with revolving squares of light. On the left was a table full of snacks and on the right another table, this time full of soft drinks. Mr Munford **STOOD GUARD** and whenever anyone reached for a bottle he snatched it away and carefully poured each drink for the pupils.

'I'm not having you *spill it* on the floor

and then falling over and **breaking a limb!'** he kept saying to anyone that would listen. (Nobody did.)

The hall was packed with people **DANCING** and excitedly chatting.

'Hey, Ted.' It was Ollie, he looked like he was wearing his **dad's suit.**

'I'm wearing my dad's suit,' he beamed.

(See, I told you.)

'Your dad is **not** a tall man is he?' I said, noticing that his suit fit remarkably well.

'Nope.'

'Looking good, Ollie,' I said, patting him on the back.

'You too, Ted. Are you ready to impress the school with your **DANCING?'**

'Erm... sure... soon,' I whispered followed by a *nervous gulp.*

'Hey, *Chloe,* can I get you a drink?'

I asked, interrupting her midway through talking to a group of girls.

'Sure.' She smiled, *taking my arm in hers!*

My heart s k i p p e d and started **BEATING REALLY FAST.** I was so happy at that moment. I needed a wee.

Two wees.

Maybe even three.

Arrggh! Why was I so nervous?

We walked over to the drinks table and joined the back of the queue. Chloe was behind me talking to **Sandra.** I chose not to get involved in their conversation. The line moved slowly but eventually I got to Mr Munford.

'Two glasses of fruit punch please, Sir,' I shouted to be heard above the loud music. Mr Munford poured me the drinks without replying. I took the cups of juice and just before I turned to hand *Chloe* the drink

I said, 'Have I told you how *amazing* you

look tonight?'

'Then why don't you give me a big, wet,

sloppy kiss?' replied Martin Harris

who was standing where Chloe should've

been.

MARTIN HARRIS!

Chloe had been so busy talking to Sandra

that the queue had moved up and, seeing

a gap, Martin Harris had pushed in and

was now standing behind me pursing his lips

ready for a **kiss!**

'Come on. If I look that amazing, I'm going

to need a big, wet, sloppy kiss.'

NOOOOooooooOOOOO!

No, No, NO, NO, NO!

NOT TONIGHT!!

CHAPTER 14

I looked around. EVERYONE nearby
had heard and was watching Martin prance
around blowing me kisses. Even Chloe was
LAUGHING.

NOOOOOOO!!!!

No, No, NO, NO, NO!

'Save a dance for me later, gorgeous.' He
laughed before running off to **burst**
some balloons, pushing people out of the way
as he went.

169

I sighed. Chloe came up and put her hand on my shoulder.

'I think I'm going to go home,' I said.

'What? We've only just got here.'

'But everyone's laughing at me. They think I'm in love with Martin Harris.'

'Don't worry about Martin. He's picking on someone else now.' We looked over, and sure enough he was attempting to give another boy a wedgie.

The music stopped and the DJ said something that was so muffled that no one could understand. It sounded like, 'Don't touch cabbages when the rabbit sings the chorus'. (But probably wasn't.)

A new drumbeat kicked in.

'Let's go and DANCE. I love this song,' said Chloe.

'DANCE? What now? I'm not sure I'm

170

ready,' I said starting to **panic** a little.

Chloe ignored my protests and grabbed my arm **pulling me towards** the dance floor. As we jostled to get enough space to dance, she whispered in my ear, 'I hope you can dance. I'd love to be crowned prom king and queen.'

'No problem.' I nodded trying to smile.

The music changed to a song I recognised and I began bopping along, instantly forgetting everything I had learned. It just wasn't happening, I was out of time and totally uncoordinated. Chloe was dancing perfectly, she was a complete natural and every song that played she seemed to know what to do. I tried copying her, but I was at least three steps behind.

I was AWFUL!

Chloe looked at me and shook her head

with disappointment. With every out-of-time arm flap and awkward leg flick she could see her prom queen crown getting further and further away. The more I tried to dance, the more **FRUSTRATED** I became in my own inabilities. The more frustrated I became, the worse I danced. Tonight was a **COMPLETE DISASTER.** The incident with Martin Harris had totally knocked my confidence. Chloe should **NEVER** have agreed to be my prom date. I was an embarrassment.

I looked to my right and Stuart Hants was dancing with Melanie Matthews and they were both dancing really well. Tonight couldn't get any worse. We were never going to be crowned prom king and queen and Chloe would never speak to me again.

Suddenly, Ollie tapped me on the shoulder.

'What's up? Why do you look so unhappy?'

'I can't dance,' I sighed.

'I can see that, Ted.'

'No, I mean I can DANCE but I can't today. I can't find my rhythm. I'm all over the place.'

'Just relax, have fun. My dad told me to dance like no one is watching.' Ollie bounded off waving his hands around and LAUGHING. He really did dance like no one was watching. I looked around. *No one was watching him.*

'Right, Ted,' I said to myself. 'Concentrate. You've got this. You need to feel the music. No, not just *feel* it you have to *feeeeeel* it. Come on. *Feeeeeeeeeeeeeel* the music.'

I listened closely to the beat and began to move in time. I let the music take over. I could *feeeeeeeeeeeel* it! I just didn't care anymore. Tonight couldn't get any worse so I might as well try to make the most of an awful situation. I moved my left arm, waved my right, spun round and kicked. Chloe had stopped dancing and was just staring at me, as were a few people around me. **I really didn't care.** Dance like no one is watching (even when everyone is watching). I channelled my inner **Henry VIII** and **ELVIS** and tried to remember everything I'd learned: a twist, a turn and spin, a leg-cross, an arm wave. Chloe giggled but stood alongside me and suddenly, instead of walking off and pretending she didn't know me, she stood beside me and began to copy my moves. As soon as she did, two or three other people also joined in.

I kept it up. I pointed left, pointed right, half turn, full turn, two steps forwards, two steps backwards, clap, hip roll, karate kick. More and more people were joining in until eventually I had the whole **DANCE FLOOR** copying my moves. I **waltzed** and w i g g l e d, quick-stepped and **LEG-WOBBLED**, tangoed and *hip-thrusted* and every move I made the crowd copied. They followed everything and they were loving it. Eventually the music stopped and the whole dance floor cheered me. *Chloe* was beaming. I was exhausted.

There was a screech of feedback from the **DJ"S** microphone and Mr Munford coughed to get our attention.

'Thank you, everyone, for coming tonight and we hope you are having a great night.'

Everyone **CHEERED.**

175

'A big thank you to the DJ...'

We all clapped.

'...and of course the dinner ladies for providing all the lovely food.'

We **CHEERED** again (even though it was far from lovely).

'It is my great pleasure now to announce the winner of prom king and queen.'

A few minutes ago I had the whole dance floor copying my moves. No one else had come close to matching my **DANCING ABILITY.** Surely I'd got this. Chloe grabbed my arm and jumped UP and down with excitement.

'The king and queen of **STAGE MOUNT SCHOOL'S** first annual prom are...

◦ ◦ ◦

◦ ◦ ◦

● ● ●

... STUART HANTS!'

WHAT?!

I mean WHAT ON EARTH?

How?
Why?
When?
Who? (No, not who, I know who –
Stupid Stuart Poo Pants Buttface)
What?

WHY?

(I know I've said why twice, but WHY?)

CHAPTER 15

How could this have happened?

To me?

To Chloe?

To Stupid Stu Hants **Poo** Pants

Buttface? (His name is getting longer.)

Tonight was the **biggest disaster**

known to man! And I should know: I can go

BACK IN TIME and see all the biggest

disasters and none of them even come

close to how much of a disaster this

disaster is.*

*Later, when I calmed down I realised that —
(1) there are worse disasters than this but at the
time it felt like the worse thing ever, and (2) I'd
overused the word disaster quite a lot in the last
paragraph.

I looked over at Chloe. She looked
genuinely upset. I couldn't believe it.
I'd tried my best but I'd let her down. I'd let
myself down, I'd even let Henry VIII and
ELVIS PRESLEY down and not a lot
of people can make that claim. I felt terrible.
Chloe shouldn't have come to the prom
with me. She should've come with with—
'STUART HANTS!' yelled Mr
Munford again. 'Stop trying to kiss
Melanie Matthews this instant. She is clearly
not interested! Go and stand the other
side of the hall immediately!

'Right, where was I? Oh yes, the king and queen of **STAGE MOUNT SCHOOL'S** first annual prom is Ted Jones and Chloe Onions!'

'WAIT! WHAT?' I screeched. 'We've won, WE'VE WON! We are prom king and queen! We did it!' I shouted at Chloe.

'Not we,' she shouted back. '**YOU!** Your **DANCING IS AWESOME!** Where did you learn those moves?'

'Henry VIII and **ELVIS PRESLEY** taught me.'

'I can't hear you,' she laughed. 'It sounded like you said Henry VIII and **ELVIS PRESLEY** taught you.'

I grabbed her hand and we went to join Mr Munford on stage. My friends high-fived us and patted us on the back as we made our way through the crowd. The pupils continued to clap as a cheap plastic crown was placed on my head and an equally tacky plastic tiara was placed on Chloe's head. I didn't care how cheap and nasty the crowns were, they meant everything to me.

'Congratulations!' said Mr Munford into the microphone. 'Ted, I had no idea you were such an accomplished performer. Will we be seeing you audition for the school show next term?'

'Well... I... ummm...' I didn't get to answer him, as Chloe pulled me by the arm. We stepped down from the stage and our friends were high-fiving and congratulating us. Once again the DJ mumbled something into the microphone which sounded like, 'The washing machine is broken and my hamsters

181

speak Russian', (but probably wasn't) and the music started up again.

Everyone turned to me and began chanting, 'Ted! Ted! Ted! Ted!' I bowed majestically and started to dance again. Two steps to the side, two steps to the other side, hip thrust, turn, slow, slow, quick-quick slow. There were classic moves from the 1500s and more elaborate moves from the 1970s. I threw in everything I'd been taught and the pupils of **STAGE MOUNT SCHOOL** loved every minute of it. They followed my every move. Chloe and I stayed on the dance floor until the very last song had ended. Mr Munford immediately turned the lights on before announcing that we should all go to the school reception as *QUICKLY* as possible where our parents are waiting to take us home. I think by then he'd had enough and wanted to get rid of us.

We found our coats and left the hall.

'That was so much fun. Thank you for being my prom date.' Chloe grinned.

'Thank **you** for agreeing to come with me. I had a great time too.'

'What do you think about what Mr Munford said?'

'What? That we should all go to the school reception as quickly as possible as our parents are waiting? He's probably right.'

'Not that... the other thing? About auditioning for the school show next term?'

'Oh, I don't know about that. I can't act.'

'You could learn. I'm going to audition. We could get the lead roles. It'll be fun.'

'I suppose I could learn to act,' I sighed. 'Although, **I'm going to need the toilet.**'

'Oh, OK, I'll wait,' she answered, gesturing towards the school toilets.

'Oh no, it's fine,' I replied. 'I'll wait until I get home.'

Well, that's it for now, but keep reading for an exclusive sneak preview of my next exciting adventure!

First there's a bit to tell you about what happens and then I'll let you read a bit of the first chapter. FOR FREE! The rest will be available soon, but you'll have to buy that. (How else am I going to afford to buy Chloe chocolates and flowers?)

Enjoy!

TED AND HIS
TIME-TRAVELLING
TOILET

SHAKESPEARE
SHAKE-UP

When Ted decides to audition for the school play, he needs to learn how to act – and fast – so, he climbs into his toilet and travels back in time to get some tips from the world's greatest playwright, William Shakespeare. Plus, there's drama as Chloe ends up in hospital, and two new classmates send Ted into a whirlwind of confusion.

Can Ted get the lead role? Who are the new classmates? What is a whirlwind of confusion? All will be revealed...

CHAPTER 1

I am a TREE.

Shhhh!

I am on the floor, crouched into a tight ball.
I am bunched up so tightly that my knees
are pressed to my nose. My knees smell
funny. I didn't know that knees even had
a smell but mine do and they smell funny
(not funny like **HAHA** but funny as in
YEUCH).

My mind wanders from being a tree and
I start to consider what knees taste like. I
stick my tongue out and have a taste. They
taste salty and **EARTHY.** Probably
because I was playing football on the field at

lunchtime and I fell over. I don't think I'll do that again. (Lick my knees, that is — not play football... or fall over. I mean, I don't want to fall over but I probably will. The chances of going my whole life without ever falling over again are slim.)

Knees don't taste as good as elbows. Did you know that all elbows taste like *strawberries?*

Go on, try it. Have a taste of your own elbow...

HAHAHA! GOT YOU! You can't do it can you? Because it's ***impossible*** to lick your own elbows.

(Aha! Don't believe me, eh? Go on, try again.)

You see. It's impossible!

If you tried this at home and you are reading this on your own then it's **a bit**

amusing, but if you are in the library
or, better still, in a bookstore deciding
if you should buy this book* now all the
other customers think you're strange
because you have your tongue out and
are trying to lick your own elbows, then
that **IS HILARIOUS!** (*You should.)

I'm just going to sit here a moment and
imagine you in a crowded bookshop, trying
to lick your elbow.

Wait... haha

Wait, not done yet... HAHA!

Hang on, still imagining it...
HAHAHAHAHAHA!

OK, carry on... no wait...

HAHA!

OK, ready now. Continue.

Now you know *that's* impossible;

however, it **is possible** to lick someone else's elbow – but I wouldn't recommend it unless you know them really well and you get them to agree to it, perhaps in writing.

The top 5 places I wouldn't recommend trying to lick a stranger's elbow

- In a queue at the supermarket (although you can always claim you were hungry).
- In the cinema (unless the film is very boring).
- In a doctor's surgery (very unwise – especially if you don't know why they're visiting the doctor).
- In the swimming pool (this is just super weird and likely to get you arrested).
- In the police station after being

arrested at the swimming pool.

SCENE: In a prison. The prisoners stand in a line

Prisoner 1: *(steps forward)* I'm Dave, I robbed a bank.

Prisoner 2: *(steps forward)* I'm Bill, I stole a car.

Prisoner 3 (Me): *(steps forward)* I'm Terry Barry Larry Gary Harry Jerry Perry Lenny Benny Johnny Tommy, Julie and I licked a stranger's elbow in a public swimming pool.

Prisoner 1: That's a weird name.

Prisoner 2 (Me): Really? After what I just told you, you think my name is the weird part?

Right, where was I? Oh yes, I'm

a TREE. I'm in drama class and everyone is pretending to be a tree. It's not the first time that our drama teacher, Mr Peters, has made us pretend to be a tree. He lowers his glasses down his nose and peers over them at us, muttering things like 'good', and 'excellent'. He rubs his small goatee beard. He looks like he is thinking but to be honest I don't think he is that interested in our interpretation of what a tree looks like in human form. I just think that it is his go-to lesson if he FORGETS to prepare a proper lesson for us. It's all very quiet as we very slowly start to move. We all imagine the sun coming out, making us grow. We stretch out our arms as if they are branches. Weird, creepy branches with hands and fingers on the end. Suddenly, Martin Harris, the school bully, jumps up and starts SCREAMING and running around the drama hall. Mr Peters immediately pushes his glasses back up to where they should be and yells at him, 'Martin Harris! What on **earth** do you think you are doing?'

'I'm a tree... AAAARRRGGHH!' he shouts, running around and flapping his arms. '... I'm a tree in the middle of a hurricane.'

A couple of people started to giggle. Mr Peters told him to wait outside the room until he'd calmed down and stopped being so silly.

Mr Peters is one of my favourite teachers. A rumour went around school last term that his first name is Peter. I wasn't sure if it was true but I started to tell people that his middle name was Peter, too. Then I told everyone that his full name is **Mr Peter Peter Peters Jnr** because I liked the idea that his dad was called Mr Peter Peter Peters and he was so happy with his choice of names that he gave his son the same name. Although none of it is true, **STAGE MOUNT SCHOOL** is the kind of place that loves a **ridiculous** rumour and they will literally believe anything.

I carry on **growing** and **stretching**, pretending my arms are branches swaying in the wind. I am very good at being a **TREE.** We are all slowly getting to full height when Mr Peters opens the door and tells **Martin Harris** to come back in and behave himself. He walks through the room shouting **'TIMBER!'** whilst pushing people over.

Mr Peters sighs, opens the door and tells Martin to leave the room again.

Mr Peters wanders amongst us and points out who is doing a good job. He nods to me and tells me *'well done,'* and, *'think about how the tree feels when the sun comes out or the rain falls on its leaves'*. I nod enthusiastically but don't give his suggestion any more thought. I think being a tree is pointless, but Mr Peters tells us that it's one of the most important exercises to master in drama. I've watched lots of dramas on the television and as yet have never seen anyone pretending to be a tree – although I did once see a dog who liked to bark.

HAHA! It's a tree joke... because of the bark... and the dog... oh, never mind!

When we are all standing up as tall as we

can get, trying to keep our balance on our tiptoes with our fingers outstretched, wiggling like leaves, Mr Peters tells us how **GREAT** we all are and then asks us to form a semi-circle around him with our chairs as he has an important announcement to make.

'Right, listen carefully, class. I have a very exciting announcement...'

(What is the very exciting announcement? Well, you'll just have to read book 3 to find out!)

ABOUT THE AUTHOR

Steven Vinacour
writes and directs
TV shows and
adverts and owns
a content creation company, creating
content for people who want content
creating.

He likes skateboarding, dogs, magic, going
to the gym, eating, and writing books about
toilets (but not all at the same time).

He can't sing, plays football badly, his
dancing abilities are questionable and he's
not very good at being an adult.

Steven doesn't take life seriously enough
and probably should know better.

GET IN TOUCH!

Ted **loves** to hear from you. If there is something you really want to know, really, **really** want to ask or really, **really**, **really** want to tell him then send him an email, and as soon as he gets back from **TIME-TRAVELLING**, he'll reply.
www.tedstoilet.co.uk
Email: **tedstoilet@mail.com**

Or follow Steven Vinacour on Instagram where you'll find news, tour dates and silliness. **@stevenvinacourauthor**

Who knows? Maybe you'll see your message or question in a future story of

READERS' THOUGHTS

'I love the book. If I had a time-travelling toilet I would go to Australia to go to the future. I mean how awesome would that be? Anyway the book is AWESOME and made me laugh more than I could ever laugh. I cannot wait till the next book.'

Rebeka

I heard that in Australia the toilets flush the other way to the rest of the world, but Ollie told me that it's not true. If you do go to Australia could you check that for me and let me know? If it does go the other way round, does that mean you go into the future not the past? Can you check that for me too? Thanks.

'I loved this book. My mum read one chapter before

bed each night and I couldn't wait to hear it. I think the author is the stinkiest author ever.' **Maya**

Hahahaha! I agree, anyone that sits around writing books about toilets must be super stinky!

'Wait! What? If I change the book to *Ted & His Amazing Super Cool and Handsome Life*, does that mean I am super cool and handsome then?' **Steven** *(the author)*

'No!'

'Hi Ted. Do you get wet socks when you flush the loo to travel to another time zone?' **Oona**

Hmm, let me ask you a question, Oona. Do you get wet socks when you have a bath or shower? No, of course you don't because you take your socks off and that's what I do. Also I can't time-travel in socks as they weren't invented until the 8th century by the Ancient Greeks and they were made out of animal hair. It wasn't until the 2nd Century AD when they started to knit socks.

'Can you travel into the future? If I could travel into the future, I would travel to 3032. I wonder if you would be there?' **Georgie**

My toilet doesn't take me to the future. But if it did, we could meet up for a futuristic lunch which would be dust that tastes of the best sweets but doesn't give you toothache, and then we'd drive a floating car that would have a special button that cures toothache and no one would ever get toothache. (I have toothache today and I think it might be distracting me — sorry about that.)

THANKS

Thank you for reading Ted's second adventure.
I really hope you enjoyed it. I love reading your
comments, and if you do get in touch I will always
reply. So why not get in touch or better still, leave a
review online or even better still get in touch AND
leave a review. Or open up your window and shout
really loudly and hopefully I will hear you – if you
live next door to me (which I don't think you do, as
my next-door neighbour is an old lady who prefers
gardening and gossiping to time-travelling toilets).

A **BIG** thank you, once again to everyone
that has helped spread the word by telling their
friends about Ted.

Thank you, of course, to Jo, Chloe and Oliver,
for reading it and checking everything. And thank
you to Fiona, Rebecca and Anna for reading it and

checking everything after Jo, Chloe and Oliver had read and checked it.

Finally, thank you to all the schools and bookshops that have invited me in. It's been great fun meeting everyone and I can't wait to get back out and meet more of you!

Don't miss **Ted's** first *AMAZING* TIME-TRAVELLING **TOILET** *ADVENTURE* in ANCIENT ROME!

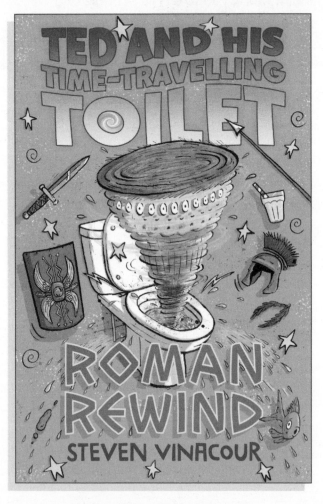

ISBN 978-1-78270-384-6